the Book of the Lion

MICHAEL CADNUM

VIKING

For Sherina

Each dawn
against the current
they sail
the white river

VIKING
Published by the Penguin Group
Penguin Putnam Books for Young Readers, 345 Hudson Street, New York,
New York 10014, U.S.A
Penguin Books Ltd, 27 Wrights Lane, London W8 5TZ, England
Penguin Books Australia Ltd, Ringwood, Victoria, Australia
Penguin Books Canada Ltd, 10 Alcorn Avenue, Toronto, Ontario, Canada M4V 3B2
Penguin Books (N.Z.) Ltd, 182-190 Wairau Road, Auckland 10, New Zealand

Penguin Books Ltd, Registered Offices: Harmondsworth, Middlesex, England

First published in 2000 by Viking, a division of Penguin Putnam Books
for Young Readers.

5 7 9 10 8 6 4

Copyright © Michael Cadnum, 2000

LIBRARY OF CONGRESS CATALOGING–IN–PUBLICATION DATA
Cadnum, Michael.
The book of the lion / Michael Cadnum.
p.   cm
Summary: In twelfth-century England, after his master, a maker of
coins for the king, is brutally punished for alleged cheating,
seventeen-year-old Edmund finds himself traveling to the Holy Land
as squire to a knight crusader on his way to join the forces of Richard
Lionheart.
ISBN 0-670-88386-7 (hc)
[1. Knights and knighthood Fiction.   2. Crusades—Third, 1189-1192 Fiction.
3. Middle Ages Fiction.]   I. Title.
PZ7.C1172Bo   2000   [Fic]—dc21   99-39370   CIP

Printed in U.S.A.
Set in Bembo

Also by
MICHAEL CADNUM

chapter
ONE

The hammering woke me—a fist pounding on the door.

A man's voice called, "Open, in the king's name!" and I could hear my master's wife telling her husband to stay still, that it was a group of traveling peddlers, swine-drunk on new wine.

But the pounding continued. I was wide awake by then, sitting up on my straw pallet, telling myself that it was certainly the miller's son. Or perhaps one of the minstrels, having a bit of riot with his companions. My pallet was beyond the dining stools and table, at the door to the smithy itself, and I stayed where I was, sure that my master could deal with this.

But then the startling music of splintering oak flung me out of bed. I offered a silent prayer to Saint Mark, the patron saint of those who would be brave.

Out in the night, a voice was calling orders, an accent of a man not from this town. I hurried into my tunic, just as my master was scurrying toward the hearth. It took a long time for the door to come asunder, and my master had the bellows working by then, the glow from the flames casting shadows.

My master thrust a straw rush into the suddenly glowing embers and called out, "Who is it? Who's knocking?" He managed to sound unconcerned, using the kindly questioning tone he used on matron and madman alike. I picked up the wood-ax, set it down, hefted the meat hook, and set it down, too. I was aware of how little I knew about fighting. The kitchen servants were stirring, and I cast aside a waffle iron and a pair of tongs, neither of them a weapon.

Maud, my master's wife, was saying this was exactly why we needed a dog. "And a big dog, too," she added, none of us really frightened yet. It was a time of outlaws and traveling beggars, and we were prepared for whatever Heaven brought our way.

I darted into the smithy, where the dark was scented with charcoal, and found what I was seeking. I hurried back into the growing light of the hearth fire, a penny maul, the hammer I used for minting fresh coins, in my grip.

Otto my master was a moneyer—a man who minted coins for King Richard. He was still trying to get a straw rush alight, blowing on the gold spark of the tip. When he had the flame alive, and had touched it to the candle ends on the hearth, he told his wife to run and tell the sheriff's men, "Outlaws are being killed by Edmund here. Hurry before they are all dead."

He said this with a hopeful smile in my direction, trusting that my duties as apprentice included knocking the brains out of outlaws. Pickpockets crowded the streets every market day, nearly every knight gone south to travel with the king to the Holy Land on Crusade. My master loved a touch of luxury, and he wore a coney-skin ruff at his church-day collar. Even though he now wore an evening robe, hastily thrown on, the gold thread gleamed. The door was pounded to kindling by then and a black glove flung the remaining scraps free of the door frame.

And then we knew this was not a brace of cowherds celebrating Monday market a few nights too soon. This was not a tavernful of drunks winning a bet by breaking into the silver mint. At the sight of the black leather armor and chain mail of our besiegers, my master Otto, Moneyer of Nottingham, drew back all the way to the far wall.

"Run!" he rasped.

I did not take a step. Even if it cost me my head, I would defend my master and his good wife.

"Edmund, run!" Otto said again, not raising his voice, the words snapping white in the cold that entered the room with the Exchequer's men.

Sometimes I hear good advice and take it, quickly. But sometimes I am slow to come to reason. "Heaven be my shield," I prayed as black ox-leather gauntlets seized me and held me hard.

My hammer dropped. Stout figures pinned my master to the wall. His good wife had not had time to hurry to the sheriff, and now looked on helplessly. The men dragged my master into the smithy, and others hauled me after him, and we panted in the blackness while these strangers lit the stub candles.

"Otto of Clifton?" said the accent, and I recognized it now, the way they spoke in London, where they prefer names like *William* and *Robert*. The Exchequer's man repeated my master's name, pronouncing *Otto* as though the name were an absurdity.

"I am Otto, and I ask who addresses me," retorted my master. I felt a dash of pride at the spirit of the man who had become, in a sense, my father.

The Exchequer's men groped among themselves. I thought for a moment that they looked for a document from the king, a proclamation, a summons to London to answer for some mistake in the Pipe Rolls, some trifling sum my master had gotten wrong. A broadsword glinted in the shifting candlelight.

"Hold him!"

Two men stretched my master's hand out along the cold iron of the anvil, his fingers splayed out white against the black. I kicked and wrestled, and though I was a mere seventeen to the full strength of these king's men, I was a moneyer's apprentice, a seasoned hammerman. The men holding me groaned with effort. A fist struck me from behind. I felt the knob of each leather-bound knuckle, a red echo of the blow in my skull. I dropped to my knees.

Strong arms pulled me erect again. The chief of our attackers, a stout, white-faced nobleman, said something in London speech. We all fell silent, the only sound Maud choking back sobs.

It took a heartbeat, no more. Steel flashed and rang against the anvil. A white, wriggling thing struggled in the char-dust on the plank floor and my master's cry was one of disbelief. Maud began to scream, and I was crying out, too, as one of the leather gauntlets picked my master's severed right hand from the coal dust. My master's cry took on a new tenor as blood pumped into the candlelight.

One of the Exchequer's men held the white thing flat against the base of the anvil while a companion drove a spike through it, like a hand of Our Lord on the Tree. The stout, white-faced leader of the men turned to me and said, "We'll have two right hands, side by side." He said this without relish, but with impatience, a man with no love for being out and around on a late winter's night.

He gave a nod and the two leather-clad men on either side of me heaved and dragged me forward. Maud struck out with a coal-poker, a span of iron like a quarterstaff. My master was bawling my name, like an animal cursed or blessed with the power of speech.

I broke free.

I bounded through the door into the dwelling quarters, and

through the splintered door, into the night. My feet were bare. I wore only my tunic, and I was glad because I could run far faster than the mail-clad, helmeted men right behind me.

They were fast, and I heard them panting from street to street, steps splashing in the runnel of water down each stone lane.

I knew the ways, and they did not, and I knew there was a nook called Grope Corner where an arrow slit in the city wall was wide enough for an eager or fearful body to worm free. I reached the slot in the stones, forced my shoulder through, but I had not attempted this since boyhood. I had forgotten my broad chest and the hammer-muscles in my shoulders.

I hung there, half in, half out of the opening in the walls. The Exchequer's men ran everywhere beyond, huffing and calling. It caused me effort, but I snaked through the fissure and fell onto the frosty grass.

I climbed to my feet and ran as a voice from the wall began to sound the alarm.

I sprinted over the star-glazed field, cursing the stitch in my side.

As I ran my tears flowed, grief over my master's agony. But in my ignorance I shed not a tear for myself. Even the sound of horsemen, three or four of them, gave me little terror.

As I ran I prayed. God sent an angel to Daniel in the lion's den, and I prayed He would send me swiftness over this dark ground.

In my ignorance of the ways of God and man I had faith that I could avenge my master's injury. I certainly believed that I could run like this forever, with the Virgin's help.

Hoofbeats grew closer. A night bird eased from the crook of an oak.

Wet clods of earth splashed on either side ahead, and the heat of the warhorse was upon me.

chapter
TWO

I dodged the steed.

But I had reached a field surface recently spread with clay-marl and lime. It was slippery, and I fell, skidding across the slick earth.

I was up at once, but the horseman rode me down, the chest of the charger striking me hard. I was slimed with white clay, and wriggled free of the hands that fought to take custody of me. They hauled me to a puddle, splashed me more or less clean. I noted well the manner of these king's men, careful that nothing happened to me, no bodily harm.

Far from being encouraged by this, I saw the care with my person for what it was: desire to enact their duty exactly, and bring me entire to their chief.

Blood reflected the candle flames. The severed hand glowed, white against the black head of the spike. I didn't look directly at it, but I saw it nonetheless, aware of it even when I looked at the dark stone wall. Heavy feet pressed me down into the cooling gore all over the wooden planks.

"Stretch out his arm," said the leader. My arm was strong, and it took three men all their effort to force it out and press it flat on the use-worn planks.

I had often imagined myself in combat, or in pain, and wondered how I would conduct myself. I did no wonderful or brave thing. I stretched the fingers of my right hand, working them, aware that they were still attached to me. I clenched my teeth.

I prayed for courage.

And then the room fell silent.

A new voice ordered us to be still.

It was an authoritative accent of my own town. The voice demanded to know who broke the king's peace on such a night. It was all formula. Even I, as ignorant of law as a tomcat, knew that with the right answer, the proper phrase delivered, the sword could do its work.

The Exchequer's man explained in his even London voice that the moneyer had been found guilty by the king's assayer of coining debased pennies. The punishment for such a felony was fit and quick, and there was already a spike, right here, through the master criminal's hand.

"And this apprentice?" was the question, and I expected to hear a fast and easy answer.

I was pulled to my feet. Geoffrey, the Lord Sheriff of Nottingham, stepped to one side to avoid the puddle of gleaming black blood.

Without looking at me he said quietly, "Put him in chains."

I was allowed to walk through the streets, up into the castle, with a guard at each side. I was permitted to remain on my feet down steps, and down further into a corridor of cold stone. A small oaken door was wrenched open with a squeal and I was wedged through the opening. These links were fresh forged, still bright with the hammer work that had shaped them.

My hands were connected to the wall with long, heavy chains, and my feet were bound into place on the floor, but these were sheriff's men manhandling me, not strangers from London, and they did their work without kicking or digging in an elbow, avoiding meeting my eye. I knew them by sight.

"Daylight comes in through the windows," said one, Henry, fat and out of breath. These were capable men, but halt or old. Most of the fit fighters had long departed to join King Richard on his holy war. The Holy Father in Rome had decreed that all who fought to take Jerusalem from the heathen would obtain indulgences—forgiveness of sins. The foulest criminal could absolve himself of wrongdoing before Heaven by joining the army of God. I envied those war pilgrims. I knew that my master was a good man, but a criminal, and that the law would consider me guilty, too.

And so would Heaven.

"And we have a she-cat who kills most of the rats," Henry was saying.

He gave my leg chain a shake of encouragement; the door creaked and slammed. A key took its time finding the slot and turning. I let my head rest against the stone. When I tried to huddle, the chains scraped along the mortared rock.

Although I could scratch the itch on my cheek, it was a laborious process, my arm weighed down with the heavy links that dragged, whispering, as I shifted them.

I had indulged in daydreams. I had visions of traveling to London once a year with my master, to sit at the Exchequer's table. Of fighting in a war against the heathen, side by side with knights. In these private glory-pageants I had imagined meeting King Richard, and serving him. Like every Christian, I longed to pray in Jerusalem. But I knew nothing of swords and lances. Worthier men than I went to fight for Our Lady.

Above all, I had dreamed of winning Elviva, who lived near the city wall. Her father was Peter de Holm, a merchant in sheep's wool, and a good friend of my master's. She had visited my master's house with her father many times, and as the two men drank Otto's Rhine wine Elviva and I shared our innermost questions about the wonders of the world, the way a witch could turn herself into a rabbit, and the power of nymphs to speak in human language. We spoke of what it would be like to meet an angel, whether he would be covered in dazzling light. Elviva leaned forward eagerly as she listened, and her green eyes brightened as she laughed. She dressed like any maiden merchant's daughter, in folds and hoods of the finest cloth, demurely, to keep the men who saw her from temptation, but her beauty was not well hidden.

Because we spoke of High Fairies and dwarves, her father thought my mind was full of lore and the simple Latin Otto had been teaching me, hoping that some day I could be, as he was, a man of worth. But Elviva and I were speaking of such things as a special language, a code safe to use. I told her that if I spied a troll I would catch him by the nose. I had begun to see myself returning from London some day with scarlet sleeves and a brocaded cap, asking to speak to her father.

Now I was where I justly belonged, before God. A pair of eyes glittered, vanished, and glittered again. The prison cat had not done her work at all well. A rat nosed the air, crept close, and peered at me. One of my first memories was of listening to my mother sing of cuckoos in Maytime while rats squeaked softly in the walls. "The old cat's been cheating her lord," I said. "Letting the likes of you dance all night."

The rat sat up, caught like a unicorn by my voice.

Daylight appeared in the high window slits, three gray stripes, and birds began their chirrup.

I stretched my arms and legs with great difficulty, the chains even heavier than before. For all the qualities of my master Otto—his welcoming smile, his gentle laugh, and his store of Frankish phrases—he had one sure defect.

He had cheated the king.

Otto had devised a way of blending Norse copper in with the silver during the smelting. "Scarcely a crime at all, Edmund," he confided. Copper was a valuable metal, too, in its way, he assured me. I think he enjoyed the art of creating the alloy as much as any increase of his own wealth. Otto bought brown ingots of the stuff from merchants traveling down from York and Whitby, and the pennies made one-fifth of copper, four-fifths of the king's silver, were as pleasing to the touch, and made the same cheerful sound bounced off a tavern tabletop, as pure silver.

Or, almost the same. I could tell the difference in smell and even taste, and certainly this debased *argentum* was less rich to the touch. But Otto had explained that the miller paid little heed to the coin that kissed his palm.

So the Devil instructs us, his eager pupils. He teases us with evil hope. The gray slashes of daylight burned brighter. They crept slowly across the stony ceiling of my chamber. The light fell upon my hand as it rested on the floor, alive with the tiny, sporting bodies of fleas.

My master was guilty, and so, as his apprentice, was I. Not that I had ever been offered a choice, and not that I had enjoyed any profit, aside from an increase in the quality of the pullets we supped on, and the quality of the ale we drank. But had I ever cautioned my master, or warned him against the wrath of the king?

The door opened, and an old man brought in a plate of brown bread and sheep's cheese, and a cup of flat beer. The bread was delicious, and the beer gone in two swallows. When I asked what had become of Master Otto, whether he lived or died, the white head shook sadly.

I prayed to Saint Peter—who had been in chains himself—that I might stay as I was for weeks or months, if it be the will of Heaven.

The slashes of daylight fell all the way across my cell and began to fade to dim russet.

Footsteps echoed, and a key rattled.

"You've business with the sheriff," said the deputy, and I recognized a kind of humor in the remark as the manacles were struck from my wrists. A man condemned to hang would be described as having business with the scaffold-builder. A man about to have his nose severed for thieving from the alms box would be said to have an appointment with a good sharp edge.

chapter
THREE

It was not quite sundown, but in this vast room it was already dark.

Candles were lit all around, a beautiful sight, with brass candlesticks, except just at the sheriff's elbow, where his wine cup awaited his touch. There a candlestick of gold—a short candlestick, but worth a knight's ransom—gave off a fine light. A whippet, a lean, white bitch, looked upon me with the mildest curiosity.

The castle was known as a place of wonders. The sheriff kept a fool, an exotic, silent creature, and the sheriff's wife was renowned as a beauty. It was said that Robin Hood himself once paid a visit within these walls.

"So here we see Edmund," said the sheriff, running his finger along a roll of vellum. I was dressed in my tunic, a smock of soft brown wool stained with my master's blood. It was a cloth few sons of freedmen were wearing, this excellent burnet, but my feet were bare.

Once again I breathed a prayer. I remained as I was, but I had eyes.

I could see no sign of a fool, and no woman at all. The Exchequer's man sat beside the lord sheriff, and I tried to read his expression. The Exchequer's man was no longer armored but dressed in finery, rich indigo sleeves. I had never seen a ceiling so high, roof beams so far above.

"This is what he is called—*Edmund,* simply that, no hamlet, no father's name?" the Exchequer's man was asking.

"His father was Arthur, a freedman," said the sheriff.

Where I found the courage to ask a question I cannot say, but the words were out before I could silence myself. "My Lord Sheriff," I said, still kneeling. "My good master Otto—does he live?"

The sheriff met my gaze. He looked worn with thought. "It's a grievous injury," he said, not unkindly. "The liver cannot keep the blood hot when so much is lost into the air."

"He's dead," said the Exchequer's man.

"I am at your mercy, Lord Sheriff. And at the mercy of our lord king." I don't know how I managed to speak in such a knightly manner at such a moment, and my voice was little more than a whisper.

"The mercy of the king!" laughed the Exchequer's man.

The sheriff rolled the parchment in his hand into a wand. "Mercy is exchanged," he said, "for acts of penance." What penance could I give, I wondered, that would earn even a single hour of mercy? The sheriff turned to listen to the whispered word of Hugh, his young deputy.

The sheriff lifted his eyebrows, reached for the silver cup at the table beside him—old silver, inset with carnelians, Flemish work—and took a sip. "You've never been on horseback, have you, Edmund?"

"Indeed, my lord, before my father and mother were taken ill with black spleen, as it pleased Heaven, I would ride to market with his wares." My father had been a cooper, a laboring man, but one of high skill, expert at carving poplar barrel wood. My father had paid for my apprenticeship when I was twelve years old by working red-eyed and weary by firelight. I had never mounted a horse in my life.

Hugh spoke again, in a low voice, and hurried from the chamber.

The sheriff turned to the Exchequer's man, his face alight, and said, "I'll offer Edmund a chance to win the favor of our king and the mercy of his God."

"But this is the son of an ignorant craftsman," said the Exchequer's man. "I'll bet you a gold mark he's never been on so much as a cob horse."

"Are you accusing Edmund of lying?" said the sheriff.

"My Lord Sheriff," I rasped. "I've a good touch with beasts, and ease their fears." This much was true—cur and hen alike enjoy my company.

Neither man spoke for a moment. "He has a crime to answer for, and I would hardly blame him for telling a lie," said the Exchequer's man at last.

"But, good Alan, you see how well he could bear a sword," said the sheriff. Even though the sheriff was uttering careful London-speech, he pronounced *swurd* like his fellow townsmen. "And an apprentice cannot be held accountable for his master's avarice."

"Of course he can," said Alan.

"But see how fit he is to battle. And what a waste it would be, before Heaven, to take such a sword arm away from God."

Alan waved a hand, like a man worried by a gnat. "Besides," he said, "if we strike off a hand he may well survive. If we send

14

him to the Holy Land against Saladin and the pagan armies, he may well never see this town again. And nearly all the Crusading men have gone, weeks past. Who'll take this apprentice townsman and turn him into a squire?"

As I was led back down the corridor of the castle, a man stood in our way, hand on his hips, feet spread, barring our passage.

He wore a sword, the iron knob of the pommel gleaming brightly.

"Ah, Sir Nigel," said the sheriff, approaching behind us. "Here you see our young man with the strength of four of the king's men. Or was it five?"

I had never seen this knight before, although I knew most other knights of the local countryside by reputation. Sir Nigel was shorter than I, although this was not unusual—I am considered tall. He had steel gray hair cut very short, like many men who go helmeted much of the time, and the whites of his eyes were faintly yellow. There was a jaundiced cast about his skin. He wore a tunic similar to mine, and if anything his was more begrimed, but with house soil, not with blood.

"This hammerman says he can ride a horse," said the sheriff.

Sir Nigel put his hand on my face, peeled down my lower lip, and felt along my eyebrow to the faint scar I have there, where a billy goat caught me as a boy.

"God can be cruel," said Nigel. "Killing my beloved squire in an accident, and leaving none to carry my shield but a liar."

"Let us keep him, then," said the sheriff. "I'll have the surgeon stand by with a poultice, something to catch the blood when the wrist is handless."

"They tell me you are called Edmund, and that you'll do anything to save your own skin," said Nigel. His tunic was soiled with duck fat and goose, a wine stain down by the hem. Like any man of quality, he kept a good table.

"Indeed, my lord, anything. Even serve God," I said.

"My choice is not so limited," he said. "There is one other youth seeking a Crusade," said Nigel. "Son of a wool merchant from the west—a man with glass windows in his house, and two chimneys." Glazed windows were very rare, except in chapels and churches. "This young man can fight, battle-ax or two-handed sword. I'll choose from the two, the winner between you and Hubert."

The knight's eyes narrowed to a laugh, and I knew my dreams were thin.

I would never manage to best a merchant's son at a game I had never played, sword to sword. And this knight, accustomed to measuring an opponent, could look into my heart.

"Be quick," said the sheriff in a low voice to the two of us. "Before the Exchequer's man has a change of heart."

chapter
FOUR

Sir Nigel walked with a slight stiffness in his stride through the evening shadows. He made his way before me through the narrow streets, past timber and clay dwellings.

Householders lingering in the streets nodded respectfully as he passed, and many gave me a glance, too. Many a sweet-faced young woman gave me a feeling look. None of them were Elviva, however, and I saw in the eyes of my neighbors the sympathy they would feel for a wretch climbing the scaffold, into the noose.

We made our way through the bakers' quarter, men who went to bed early so they could rise and knead their dough into bread by morning. We left the city gates, the guards there saluting us with cheer. The late winter fields were green, the trees bare and bronze in the setting sun. Sir Nigel and I approached a walled living-stead beyond the town.

The knight pushed open a large wooden gate studded with bronze points. We paused in a small, clay-paved courtyard before a house of blue stone. I had seen this place from the road, one of the few stone dwellings in the countryside. It had belonged to Sir

Roger, an old knight, war weary from a Crusade long past. The old knight had died of a flux, bleeding from his guts, some six months past. This was the new tenant of Roger's hall.

Horses nickered from the stables at the sound of the knight's voice. We stopped in the door yard.

"Take a stance," he said in London speech.

I understood what he was saying, *tan a strythe*. My heart was beating fast as I planted my feet, held my head at an angle, jaw set, as I had seen knights do on tournament day.

Nigel walked around me, a man studying a bullock he had led from market. I knew what was coming, but it was still a shock when he charged into me and knocked me flat.

I jumped to my feet.

"Try again," he said.

I was down at once as he struck me with only one fist, swung backhand, a blow I had seen coming. He did not offer me a hand to help me up, nor did I expect or deserve one.

"Your master Otto was a thief," he said at last.

"No, my lord, he was an honest coiner."

The knight gave a laugh, but there was sadness in the sound. "Again," he said.

This time he barely touched me, a quick stab of his open hand, below my ribs. I gasped, swore to myself I would not go down, and fell.

I was on my feet in an instant—shocked at myself, ashamed. I was in angry tears.

"You won't defame my master Otto," I heard myself say. "Or his good wife."

The knight laughed. "I'll do all of that, Edmund. Ride the wife to market, and you looking on, if it pleases me. I'm making a mistake, I am afraid before the saints. I'm making a terrible mistake to let a thief's apprentice sit at my table. But it is a blunder I am making with my eyes open."

I hated him.

The knight showed me into a great hall with oak beams in the ceiling, and a graceful figure I took to be a pleasure-woman offered him a cup.

Straw was thick all over the floor, and servants appeared through the hearth smoke, unbuckling Nigel's sword. Beyond, a large fireplace gave off cheerful firelight, with the oblong shapes of hams and haunches festooned over the oakwood smoke. Nigel sat with a sigh and nodded that I should join him. I took a long look around, hoping for—and fearing—a sight of this Fighting Hubert.

The bench Nigel indicated for me was a well-planed piece of oak, better than any my master had possessed. Knights were renowned for their enjoyment of manly appetites, women, food and drink. I had been living in the household of a minter, however, and while we had enjoyed nothing like the finery of the sheriff, we had drake for midday meal, and the whitest bread.

The table knife was decent silver, wood-handled, and heavy. I longed to tell Elviva where I was. This knight watched every move I made as I accepted a warm bread trencher with a slab of beef from a broad-shouldered manservant.

"Wenstan," said Nigel to his man. "Edmund here thinks he can better Hubert in combat. And Edmund here has carried neither sword nor buckler in his life."

"Hubert?" said Wenstan, as though the idea stunned him. "Oh, I don't—" He stuttered over his words. "I don't think that would be a fair contest at all, my lord."

"We'll see tomorrow," said Nigel, as though it mattered nothing to him, either way. "But we can't have Edmund riding forth naked to have his head stuck onto a pike, can we?"

Naked, to men-at-arms, means unarmored. A messenger, even an archer, however well-appointed, was naked in the eyes of an armored man.

The cup Wenstan served me was heartwarming red wine. "Oh, my lord, we'll have Edmund caparisoned like a Templar," said Wenstan. In conversation, anyone of much greater quality than oneself was addressed as *my lord,* even, if the case arose, *my lord king, my lord pope.* I noted that Wenstan did not refer to me as "Master Edmund," or "squire."

I was still in my blood-dyed burnet, cloth of quality, but I was alive to the fact that the serving man wore the best sort of brass buckle on his belt, and a knife with a buck-horn handle.

"Hubert is out riding," Nigel said. "Running down a vixen, I would guess. He has new chain mail and a barely used saddle. He's getting used to the feel of the leather."

I chewed and worked hard to swallow the suddenly flavorless meat in my mouth. I was sorry when Wenstan left us alone.

"I would have left to join our king on the Holy Crusade long before this," Nigel was saying, "but sick as I was, I could not stand up or leave my bed."

"It grieves me, my lord, to hear it," I said.

Nigel swallowed wine and considered me. He said, "A hammer killed my squire."

This could only be a poor omen, or an ugly coincidence. Before I could think of how to ask after this misfortune, he added, "It was a stonemason's mallet, dropped from the chapel of Saint Bartholomew, not five weeks past. Knocked out his brains and all his senses. He died."

It did seem unnecessary to add that a youth with neither brains nor senses could not live, but I expressed myself as my master had taught me. I said I was sorry to hear of my lord's loss.

"I will not refer to him again," said the knight. "It pains me."

"As it pleases you, my lord."

"I had a dream," said the knight, "and after waking, I told it to the lord sheriff over wine yesterday. I dreamed the man who killed my squire rose from the dead and came to see me, offering his service. I spent hours wondered how such a thing could come to pass."

I kept my eyes downcast.

"I killed the mason for his bad luck," said Nigel. "Climbed up the scaffold, cut his throat, and paid the master mason a bag of silver pennies for the loss. Real silver," he said pointedly, "with old King Henry's face stamped in them."

I kept my mouth shut, scratching flea bites on my legs.

"You'll need beef to give you strength," said Nigel. "Perhaps you aren't a bad youth, in your heart. I was a muscular lad like you once, and with no more sense than a duck. I have killed three men in my life, Edmund. One by accident, only my second tournament, braining a knight from Poitou with the flat of my sword. One a yeoman goose thief I ran down and skewered—" Nigel stabbed the wooden trencher-board with his knife—"through the spleen, so he bled bright red. And just recently this star-cursed mason's apprentice."

A trip to the Holy Land to fight for the True Cross absolved a sinner of even the worst crimes in the eyes of Heaven. Still, I was surprised that such a seasoned warrior had not taken many more lives.

"Before I die," he was saying, his eyes bright, "I pray to serve Our Lord in one great battle."

"God wills it," I said in a soft voice, unthinkingly echoing the Crusader's cry.

Nigel slapped the table, laughing, his eyes keen. This knight's gaze had a powerful charm—I could not help liking him now. "Maybe you have a counterfeiter's heart, and a Christian's liver."

The liver, I knew, was the seat of courage, but I was not braver nor more cowardly than any other man.

"I have every penny ever paid to me here in this house," the knight continued, giving a leather pouch of silver at his side a squeeze. "Ready to give to serve the saints."

The touch of the silver at his side seemed to set him dreaming, as the feel of money will. No doubt a true squire would have said something wise and worldly, but the wine had made me stupid.

He peered at me. "You're weary!"

"Never, my lord."

I trailed behind Sir Nigel, my attention caught by a distant sound.

Perhaps that step rustling the floor straw in the distance was Hubert, back from the hunt.

How long would it take Hubert to beat me into the mud with his sword?

chapter
FIVE

"You'll sleep here," said the knight.

I thanked him. This soft blanket and feather-padded bedroll would be undeserved luxury.

"I'm awake and about well before dawn," the knight was saying. He caught his breath and took a step back.

I blinked around through the candlelight, to see what could have startled this man-at-arms.

A spider fingered upward along the wall above my bedding.

Sir Nigel seized a stool. He took a back swing, about to flatten the tiny trespasser against the stone.

"If I may, my lord," I said. I reached out, and the black, glittering thing hurried away from my touch. But I was persistent, and trapped it, cupping it in my palm.

The spider was busy in the folds and wrinkles of my cupped hands. I hurried through the hearth smoke and let the many-legged creature free outdoors, into the night.

When I returned to my bedding I found clothing folded neatly, and a belt with the best brass buckles, and shoes of the sort swordsmen wear, studded with iron. But there was no weapon, not even a short sword.

I lay still while, in the far recesses of the hall, Wenstan snuffed out the few flickering candles and collected the stubs. I thought I heard the sound of lust at work, a pleasure-coupling somewhere in the dark. I put my hand to my throat, feeling the place where Hubert's blade would sever my voice and wind.

At an early hour, some nameless time after midnight, when the huge dark chamber of the hearth was a single glowing spark of red, I left my bed. If there was a night guard I could not see him. Someone snored. A male voice muttered something in a dream. All sound of rut and pleasure was quiet.

Step by step I took myself across the hall. I held my breath, all around me wine-soaked sleepers.

Nigel lay flat on his back, hands at his side, looking like the effigy of a knight on a tomb except that he was naked, his sleeping face youthful in the dim light. A posset cup gleamed dully on the floor, a marriage of wine and honey some men keep beside them in the night.

Perhaps I hoped some burly man servant, some sleepless wench, would accost me. I felt a pair of eyes on me, but when I turned there was no one.

My new clothing fit me well enough, although the shoes were a little large, and stiff, creaking with every step. It was all new, sleeve and collar, and I wondered at the knight's generosity, endowing a fledgling like myself.

I slipped to the heavy wooden front door and gave it a nudge, and then a push, and then at last put my full weight into it. What made me certain, at that moment, that someone spoke my name?

But I could see no one.

I kept my gait deliberate as I crossed the courtyard. A horse made a high note of inquiry, shifting its weight in the stable. The courtyard gate groaned. Surely it would wake the household.

Careful to carry myself like a man about his master's business, I left the dwelling-stead and found myself on the road, a track of rutted dirt through frosty fields. The scent of rain reached me from the north, the moon dirty with cloud.

As I walked I groped into my soft-spun blouse and pulled out a slack coin purse. I teased open the mouth of the leather bag, and out spilled three quartered silver pennies, glittering under the dim moon.

One of them fell to the earth, and I knelt, retrieving it from among the deep, uneven ruts. It was a neatly quartered King Stephen penny. I had been careful to take only these few cut coins, despite the other sacks of silver in Sir Nigel's chamber. My hope was that I could stay at large long enough to find a future as a laborer. I could mend gates or hammer roof pegs.

If I found my freedom. And if I, over time, made my way back to Elviva, with silver I had earned with my two hands . . .

I found my stride, into the fringes of forest, where farmland sliced into the oak woods.

Past the roofs of sleeping cottagers, past pens of sows and hen-houses boarded against foxes, the spine of the high road bore me on its rise and fall toward country I had never seen before. I had never drawn a breath which was not owed to my father or my master, and now I was indebted in all ways to my new lord, the knight. As I walked I felt the long leash tighten around my neck, my deceit. The high way had been gouged by cartwheels and wagons and pocked by the hooves of dray horse and ox, and sometimes I nearly stumbled in my new shoes.

I grew icy at the sight of the strange fields as they closed around me, and yet it was not fear of other, less reluctant robbers than myself that slowed me to a standstill. It was certainly not fear of the most famous robber, Robin Hood, that had me standing in the mountainous ruts of the king's road, hesitating.

I was betraying my father's last words to me: "Be proud, Edmund." Proud meant virtuous, above any thought of wrongdoing. His breath so thick in his throat the words were like ice breaking underfoot, his lips ash-black and cracked.

But I continued to trudge forward, past geese pens and thick stands of young trees destined to be the roof supports for peasant homes.

I had never been so far from town.

Rain began to patter on my shoulders, soaking the hair of my head, making me regret that I wore no hood or cap. It was not long before the cold rain was so thick I could not see three steps before me.

I slipped on the mucky road, and cursed it. My new shoes sucked at the mud, stuck to it, each step lifting with a loud smacking sound, followed by a splash as I forged ahead. The road was slippery as goose grease, and I staggered.

I stumbled sideways, twisting my ankle.

I am not hurt, I thought, bent over with the effort of lying to myself.

My right foot was numb, that sharp painlessness that sickens the heart.

"It's not so bad," I said aloud.

I lumbered across the muddy track, into the hazel-wood saplings along the road. Soon, I promised myself, I'll be on my way again. I just need to rest for a moment.

Wind gusted, and the rain weakened, stopped entirely.

A fox barked, a quick *snick-snick.*

chapter
SIX

I woke behind a wall of stone and thorn.

A mist rose off the meadow, sunlight strong above, birds loud. A herd of cows somewhere far off bawled and lowed, and the air was earthy with the smell of wood smoke and manure.

The sun was beautiful. My foot throbbed. I was weak with hunger, my throat dry. Birds took sight of my blue squire-cloth and scolded each other, fluttering. I peered through the leafless shrubs. When I stood on my swollen foot I could hobble like the cripple who performed on market day, a sleight-of-hand artist, making hen's eggs vanish at a touch.

The roof of a peasant's cottage thrust above the thorn shrubs, a low thatch and cob-clay building, greenwood spewing smoke through a gap in the roof. Walking took a long time, my shadow lurching ahead of me like a hunchback.

The sight of a small flock of geese marching from the interior of the dwelling awakened memories of fat sizzling in a fire, steaming slices of meat on a wooden platter.

A well-fleshed young woman was driving the birds, dressed in hairy gray wool, a kerchief tied over her hair. At the sight of me she stopped.

"Good morning to you," I said.

She made no reply.

Then she lifted one corner of her mouth in a cautious smile. Travelers were common on the road, and even peasant's sons were known to take to the King's High Way toward distant regions. A peasant who remained at large for a year and a day was no longer bound to the land; the towns were crowded with freedmen begging for their bread.

The geese stretched out their long necks and bore down upon me, braying as they came.

"Away," I cried, in my most commanding voice. "Stand away from me!"

I scrambled onto the wall, balancing on my good leg, and the lord gander extended his neck and gave my new shoes a pinch. "Call off your geese, if you will," I said.

The goose girl was pretty enough, and she seemed to enjoy the sight of a townsman in well-made clothes kicking at a large, hissing gander. The other geese were honking, trumpeting, blaring. The cottage door lurched open and a short, smoke-grimed men stepped forth into the sunlight, carrying an ax. He was gray-haired and thick-necked, and had not taken the time to put on his cap.

The young woman approached me with without a further smile or a single word, stooping to pick up a slender stick. The gander nipped at my legging, and then seized the skirt of my tunic and would not let go, even when I kicked hard and accurately despite my injury, feathers, goose down, and goose dust drifting up into the air.

The peasant with the ax brandished it in my direction, bawling some imprecation, but by now I was ready to battle. I jumped from the wall, and gave the gander another solid kick. The bird spread his wings and ran around me in a crazy circle, sounding his alarm, the other geese honking, too, giving their champion and myself fighting room even as they seemed to grow greater in number, geese and goslings everywhere.

The axman parted them easily, and in his wake the geese settled, rearranged their feathers, suddenly matronly and gossipy. The axman seized the gander by the neck and examined its wing, stretching it out while the gander scolded and hissed. He examined the stem and stern of the gander without uttering a sound or releasing his ax.

Then the peasant let the bird go, and the gander sprinted with his wings half-cocked to the head of his retreating army. The geese swept along in the direction the young woman indicated with her long yellow switch, a tide of white and brown motley birds, bickering and celebrating.

The peasant fixed me with his eye—*You stay here.* Then he hurried to the young woman, caught up with her, and pushed her hard, without a word, sending her full length into a puddle. He kicked her, a full-strength, bone-ringing blow. It was as though this fieldman was demonstrating to me, *This, sir, is a kick.*

Before I could stop myself I was at the man's side, my hand on him. I meant no injury, but shook him by the shoulder, as one might shake a dreamer, urging him from a nightmare. He pushed me away. One part of my mind cautioned me to bid him a good day and leave.

But he gave me another push, one that reminded me of Sir Nigel. I hit the peasant with my right hand, without putting much effort into it, a slap.

The man fell hard, and sat there gaping at me. He groped for his ax, and leaped to his feet.

His glance searched my garb, mud-freckled dyed wool and

new buckles, wondering what a young man would be doing, out so far from town without so much as a palfrey to carry him. And without so much as a small-sword in his belt. With a right hand that could strike as well as any smith's.

He called something to the goose girl, words I could not make out. She fled back to the cottage, shouting. The sound took me back to the mornings of my boyhood, when country dwellers would greet each other across the open land with a shout, cowherds and craftsmen alike, each with his own way of giving voice to a greeting.

"I'll pay you a quartered cross-penny for a loaf, if you please," I said. "And a wedge of cheese."

The man put a finger to his chin. A silver penny was a year's plow-alms, a year's tax on a team of oxen. A quarter-penny was no small amount of money. By offering silver for a common meal I was close to gibbering like a madman—or a man in flight from the law.

The lusty cries of the young woman had brought a young man her age from the confines of the house. He ran hard toward her, carrying what looked like a clay-cutter, a blade designed to slice earth for cottage walls. The young man spoke briefly with the young woman and took off across the land yelling some alarm in peasant speech. The young woman hefted her skirts and sprinted off in another direction, calling, "An outlaw, an outlaw!"

As this cry drifted through the morning sun, the axman realized that it was too late to charge me the price of a prize bull for a cup of beer. Field folk were running from far around.

I brushed the axman aside and breathed a prayer. I ran painfully as fast as I was able through green goose-mud to the cottage and stepped inside.

30

Thick smoke stung my eyes, and the heavy, sour funk of long human habitation. A half-moon of black bread sat on a platter, beside an earthen pitcher. A wife in coarse-spun cloth stood before an infant's bunk, the babe squirming pink in the shadow. The wife held a pitchfork, and defended a kid goat with the sweep of her skirt. The kid frisked in place, held by a tether.

The brave wife stayed as she was, work-polished wooden fork level at me. She watched as I drank deeply of barley beer and tore off a healthy chunk of bread. Chewing fast and swallowing, I left one of my quartered pennies on the soot-caked firestones in the middle of the room.

The axman was waiting for me, but at his wife's cry, "Silver!"—*Selfer!*—he leaned on his ax. He said something I did not understand.

And then I worked out his heavy accent, each word becoming clear in my mind. I scampered away, geese flapping and honking before me.

Hurry.

A knight is coming.

I hobbled through the dew-thick grass to the crest of a low hill, and turned in the warm morning sun. A charger, the best sort of warhorse, was in full gallop, heading right toward me. The steed shook his head, foam flying, his mane tossing in the sunlight, brass jingling. I stood my ground.

His rider, a young knight, dragged and sawed at the reins. The horse jigged sideways, its belly wet, its flanks spiky with moisture. I put out one hand and caught the bridle as the horse thundered past, all heat and sweat, tossing and snorting. The knight was a young man I had not seen before, his face screwed into a grimace.

"Hoo!" I cried. At this word from me, the steed rolled his

eyes, flattened his ears, and began to run in a straight line, back down the hill.

"Hoo," I repeated, in a lower, more strangled voice, hanging on, dragging like a rag puppet through the grass.

The animal circled back, slowing down. His great hooves, splashed and glistening, slowed to a trot and then a walk, as my injured leg throbbed. The rider jounced, hauling on the bridle, and when the horse stood still at last the young man fell, over the horse's neck, down into the grass.

"Great terror!" said the young man when he could make a sound. *Grete terrour,* an accent from the west. "That horse fills me with dread."

He wore new mail, the fabric of close-woven iron gleaming, link to link. His helmet was stout bullock leather, and he worked to get it off, shaking his blond hair, sitting up.

At his side was a broadsword. "Give me the silver," he said, still breathless.

I hesitated. *Climb onto the horse,* said an inner voice.

Ride hard. Escape.

"Give me the silver you stole from Sir Nigel," said the young man. "The king's men are coming, and they want to skin you."

I held out my hand. "I am Edmund," I said, as though we had all day to share courtesies. "And you—?"

He gripped my hand with his leather glove, and said, "I am Hubert."

The black, mounted figures of the king's men gathered at the edge of the pasture, letting their mounts breathe. They rode at an easy pace toward the sun, fanned out, encircling us.

Hubert hefted the slack bag of silver in his hand, and took a moment to tie it to his belt, beside the pommel of his sword.

"Good morning to you," said Alan to Hubert, ignoring me entirely.

Alan let his horse take a few easy paces, until his pale, tight face looked down at me, blocking the sun. "Sir Nigel said you and Hubert were sporting," he said. He let me see the way his eyes took in the sack of silver beside Hubert's belt. "Hunting roebuck."

"And making a poor game of it," said Hubert.

Alan let me see how well he knew everything, giving me a colorless smile. "Without a crossbow," said Alan, "with only one horse, one of you lame. I would say the morning has gone badly."

Alan's steed gave a shake of his bridle, black leather with fittings of polished copper.

"Your master would be grateful," said Alan, "in weeks to come, if we sheared off the hand of this walker-in-the-night, and let him bleed out on this very spot."

"My lord, it may be as you say," said Hubert. "But Sir Nigel believes that both of us are under his protection, and would see the least harm to any one of his men to be an assault upon his own body."

Alan laughed, letting us watch him count us with his eyes, and count the dozen figures of his own men.

Hoofbeats approached. A heavy horse flung mud. A leather and iron armored figure approached. This horseman carried a war helmet by his side, a square bucket with eye slits and a socket for a plume. This upside-down helmet swung heavily, plumeless, a great dent in its side.

Our newcomer was yet another man I had not seen before,

soiled with house smoke, bearded, with a startling sneer across his face. In addition to a war helmet, he bore a hunting lance—not as long and heavy as a tournament lance, but fit to run down boar or bear. Or, indeed, an armored man.

This stranger pulled up, and did not speak, letting his mount crop grass while he took in the sight of us, his teeth gleaming, lance upright in the sun. His horse lifted its tail and manured the earth with bright, steaming turds.

Alan straightened in his saddle, and the Exchequer's men drew together into a cluster.

"Save your steel for the Pagan," Alan said with a thin laugh, pronouncing it *Paynim*. "All of you—when you fight side by side with this counterfeiter's apprentice."

chapter
SEVEN

The wind blew cold, white clouds casting shadows over wood and field. Cows turned their backsides to it. The breeze brought tears to my eyes.

The ride back was not long enough—I wished I could forestall my return for many hours. As I rode behind Hubert I could feel the tense strength of his small frame. The horse tossed and pranced, turning his head to gaze at the two of us, showing the white of his eye.

Hubert struggled, scolding the mount in a quiet voice, and this caused the animal to kick his hind hooves so that I had to hang on to Hubert to keep from tumbling into the road. "Three days I've been riding Winter Star," said Hubert. "Look how he tries to turn his head around and bite me!"

It was true that Winter Star was trying to snake his muzzle around, baring his strong yellow teeth. What I feared more than the warhorse was the glance of the knight who rode with us, the bearded fighting man with the scarred mouth.

"Who is he?" I asked, softly, directly into Hubert's ear.

"He is Rannulf," said Hubert.

I knew the name.

When we reached the courtyard of the hall, Wenstan watched while Hubert tended Winter Star. Rannulf remained on horseback and watched for a while, and then when I glanced back he had vanished.

With Rannulf's disappearance, Wenstan whistled a minstrel tune under his breath, a pretty tale, the story of a man who felt love for a woman he could never see, who lived behind a wall. "The white thread and the red thread," sang Wenstan. He did not stutter when he sang.

Winter Star grew calm under the stroke of Hubert's comb. I tried to make my question sound casual. "I thought Christians were forbidden to speak to a man like Rannulf."

Hubert jumped back as the horse swung its head around to eye the two of us. The air rang with the sound of chain mail under the fettler's hammer, blacksmith's smoke drifting over the courtyard. "No one talks to him. And Wenstan says we should not speak *of* him," said Hubert.

"He killed five men in the famous tourney of Josselin, didn't he?" I persisted. Tournaments had been condemned by the church. Father Joseph, who preferred homilies on Mary feeling the Babe leap within her womb, had said that such mock battles were an offense to Heaven.

"Wenstan says six knights were killed that day," said Hubert. "A game-fight that became a battle. Rannulf has been ordered on Crusade by the priests, but he has not yet decided to go. Wenstan says he cares nothing for his soul."

To have no regard for one's soul was like caring nothing for one's mother—it was impossible to imagine a man so callous or wicked. But some knights had a reputation for beating women senseless, stabbing drunks, running down eyeless beggars, all to expend their idle energy. My master Otto had said this was why the Crusade was required, not merely to free Jerusalem from the Saladin's armies, but to send fighting men far from the marketplace.

"Sir Nigel lets him share the roof with us—"Hubert fell silent as Wenstan approached, singing softly about the red lily and the white.

Wenstan wrapped my foot in yellow linen, cross-binding it so I could stand with and stride with ease, but all the while I wanted to ask about this knight who defied the power of the Church. The sword Wenstan brought out from the dark interior of a side room was long and tarnished, with a grip of cured cowhide. He extended the pommel in my direction, and I hesitated.

Wenstan nodded impatiently.

Still, my hand held back.

"If you look like a squire," said Wenstan, with difficulty, "if you look fighting-able, you may win our lord Nigel's heart."

I had never held a sword, and I was surprised at how well it fit my hand. And yet, when I gave a cut at the empty air, I felt the strangeness of the weight, my body out of balance. Wenstan gave me a smile and shook his head.

Someday, I swore to myself, I'd use a sword to whisk an infidel's blade from his fist, chop off the hand, the arm, and the head. With Nigel, Rannulf, all of them, looking on amazed.

Winter Star grew stoical at my touch, as I dabbed tree tar onto a cut on her knee, caused, Hubert said, by the horse running through the woods. "The horse was hoping I'd be brained by a branch. Which I was, nearly." He had me feel a bruise like a dove's egg at the crown of his skull.

I sat at a stone wheel, working the pedal myself, grinding sparks from my age-gray sword. The housemen accepted my presence among them, as I took my time, happy to have my hands at work. I mended a girth-strap, to sling under a horse's belly, as I understood it, and hold the saddle where it belonged. I reworked a new buckle for a hasp for one of the pleasure-women's ivory lockets.

The household brought me metal work, ivory crosses dangling by a frail link, tinker's pots cracked after only the second boiling. All the servants save Wenstan were to travel to other masters once Sir Nigel left on Crusade. Only a few would remain to husband the place in its emptiness and keep beggars and outlaws from taking roost.

It was understood by all that to leave for Crusade was to travel to one's death—few Crusaders expected to return. There was sadness as well as eagerness to make things right in the air all afternoon, into the evening. The word was about that a moneyer's apprentice and a hammerman was available, no work too fine. I blushed to mend the love lockets of the brazen ladies, keeping my hands alive so my thoughts could sleep. The cook's carving knife needed a new rivet, a medallion of Our Lady needed a hook-and-hook, an easy way to attach a necklace, and strong, if the work is well wrought.

Late in the day, when it was almost too dark to mend the bucket handle in my hands, Hubert leaned into the smith's shop and said, "Sir Nigel sends for you."

chapter
EIGHT

Nigel sat at his table, paring a green apple.

At his elbow was a document, walnut ink letters on parchment.

"This fruit should have been cider months ago," Nigel said, handing me half the fruit, peeled entirely of its skin.

I sat and took a bite of the mealy flesh.

"Alan de Roche, the Exchequer's man, has changed his mind," said Nigel, giving a nod toward the paper on the table. "It seems Alan suspects there is a hidden trove of silver unaccounted for in your master Otto's household. Dig and pry as they may, Alan is surprised at your master's cunning. If Rannulf had not found you this morning, you would be in chains again, with hot coals being applied to your privy parts."

"It was a blessing that Sir Rannulf discovered me," I said.

"A blessing?" He picked a fleck of apple skin from his tongue with some delicacy. "Perhaps. But it was no accident."

"Then I owe you my continuing thanks," I said, my voice trembling.

The fire spat and sighed in the hearth.

"Indeed you do. The law is a knot. You are mine, now, breath and bone. If I want you."

"I am your servant," I offered.

He laughed. "Don't be so sure you could master Hubert in a fight," he said. "Small creatures can have great strength."

"Like a spider, my lord," I said.

"Or a cutpurse," said Sir Nigel.

The night was cold, even in the hall.

"Do you see what's missing? Scan this writing, Edmund, and tell me what's not here."

How deliberate writing is! How insistently it races across the page, and just as demandingly takes up again, top to bottom, bristling with command.

"Even a cat could see what is not there, my lord," I heard myself say. "The letter has no seal."

Nigel smiled. "It's a warrant without the king's seal. The king is in Italy, or Crete, or in Acre itself by now, Heaven willing. Alan thinks he can winkle you into his tong-and-coal confessional, where you'll tell him anything he wants to know."

"You'll keep me to spite the Exchequer's man?" I asked hopefully. "And keep Hubert, too," I asked, equally hopeful. "Do you need two squires?"

"God's blood," said Nigel, almost a happy prayer. Every Christian was warned against swearing by Jesus's limbs, and His face and His bodily fluids. And yet, I wondered—who could know more about the stripes and spear stabs of Our Lord than a knight-at-arms?

"I like you, Edmund, because you have a lively glance, a fair appearance, and a strong arm." He smiled. "Besides, a man can use two of everything," said Nigel.

That night the hall did not sleep. Dozens of candles burned bright, the perfume of beeswax in the air. Tanner's wax was rubbed into straps, spear points filed to a shining point. Wenstan gave commands, and the shadows of servants flowed across the straw-covered floor. Sir Nigel sat in a corner, reading and conferring with a man-of-law, writing down instructions, and, most important, creating a will.

"Shouldn't you and I write down our wills?" said Hubert.

"I own nothing," I said. Only my bones and my blood, I did not add.

Hubert had trouble folding all of his belongings into the way-pack, and I helped him. "This is a sprig of rue from my mother's garden," he said. "I promised to bury it near the Holy City. And here is a pendant my father gave me, in the shape of the Holy Cross. You see the little glass window—I'm to put a stone from the Holy City inside, and bring it back."

I left the courtyard gate in the darkness, and passed the midden, curs snapping and growling over kitchen bones. I emptied a bucket of slops, urine and solid waste, onto the steaming heap.

From a distance the hall was a stern place, its roof squared off, glints of firelight through the window slits. And tonight this countryside was even more bleak, only a few stars in the sky behind a caul of cloud. A north wind, I thought, with a promise of more rain.

I glanced around, alive to the fact I was being watched. But there was no one, only the hedge mice scurrying, and the great oaks, lifting branches toward the night sky.

I found myself wishing my mother and my father could see me as I was now, among Crusaders. Or that Elviva could see me.

But it was true—I did hear a step. And another, someone close.

I spun, and Rannulf had me by the arm. Startled, I dropped the slop bucket.

"I owe you thanks, my lord," I said, when I could speak.

Most knights shaved their beards, and kept their heads round-cropped. Rannulf had a short, dark beard, and his hair was a tangle. The night was too thick for me to see the color of his eyes, but they caught the dim light and reflected it.

He thrust a heavy iron object into my hands. My hands searched the cold iron of his helmet, and found the grievous dent.

A blacksmith's maul in one hand, the other holding an iron-smith's tool, I plied my might against the stubborn dent. A small crowd could not keep itself from gathering, as word got around that although it was near midnight I was working to reshape the helm of Sir Rannulf.

Rannulf's eyes were pearl gray, and he folded his arms and watched me, leaning against the workshop bench. Few veteran swordsmen did not have a healed gouge or lopped finger on the shield side of their bodies. The scar above Rannulf's mouth gave him a permanent sneering look, but his gaze was not unfriendly.

The iron had been fire-forged, and as I labored I was aware of the absurdity of my attempt. The blow that had caved in this strong helmet had been a master-stroke, delivered by a battle-ax or a mace. How could I, not even an apprentice at arms, begin to equal the force of such a blow?

Rannulf watched without a word. As I hammered sweat seeped into my eyes. My grip grew numb. My ears, blow by blow, went half deaf, the only sound the ringing of my hammer on the peen, a long steel chisel with a round knob instead of a blade. Work as I might, I accomplished nothing.

You're not equal to this, staver's son, said a sour voice in my heart.

Rannulf met my eyes. He made no sound, but his eyes flickered from me, to the helmet, and back.

I could not believe what I was hearing when he spoke, softly, in an even voice, his words clear despite the scar along his lips.

He said, "God give you strength."

God's strength. It was a phrase Father Joseph used, encouraging my father as he faced death. Perhaps, I thought, Rannulf is not such a prayerless man after all.

My tool struck sparks. My hammer found its rhythm, driving the injury out of the helmet, until it was whole.

chapter
NINE

We rode into town early the next morning, all of us having spent a hectic and sleepless night, and, in the company of the priest, confessed our sins.

Afterward, outside the church, a crowd of our neighbors gathered. My master's wife—his widow—Maud swept me into her arms, a long, breath-stopping hug.

"Don't worry about me, Edmund," she said. "I'll be living with my brother and his wife, with God's blessing."

Every week Maud loaded a basket with loaves and cheese and delivered it to the almshouse, where the poor and sick took shelter. She told me once that helping a bereft person was like helping Christ Himself. While always quick with her opinions, she viewed the world through the impatient cheerfulness of her own spirit. I could not meet her eyes just then, hoping she did not think me a great sinner.

"You were Otto's right hand," she said. "But a hand has to obey its master."

"The saints protect you," I said, tears in my voice.

With the cheering of the throng, I could not hear what Maud

was saying as I pulled myself nervously into the saddle. And then I saw Elviva.

How is it that some women give every gesture a kind of beauty? Even in waving farewell, Elviva was graceful, one hand to her throat to keep the shawl in place against the chill. We had met in the market some forenoons, and walked into the sun near the churchyard, sharing our hopes. She had told me once that she prayed to Our Lady to bring her a husband with a strong arm and a full heart. I told her that her prayers matched mine.

When I reached down to take her hand the warhorse displayed a surprising patience, shaking the bridle, tossing his head, but standing quiet as I tried to find words. Elviva's father, the wool-man, and her mother, a thin woman with a sweet smile, looked on, little dreaming how much Elviva and I felt for each other. Perhaps as a Crusader returning from the wars—in the unlikely chance that I survived—I would have some new status in the eyes of a merchant.

Winter Star watched the other mounted riders make way ahead, and trotted to join them, tossing his mane. Elviva ran along with me, as I tried to control the horse and failed. I was a little frightened of the noble charger, as though I rode upon a lion, and felt a certain gratitude toward him. Only in my dreams had I ever sat upon such a steed.

At last Winter Star and I left Elviva behind.

We were a "right gang of worthy men," as Nigel put it. A rooting pig from one of the nearby households scampered, un-hindered by its hugeness, caught up in the festivity. Men and women both wished us Godspeed as we clattered up the cobbled street through the city gates.

Hubert perched on a new, black mount named Shadow, with a soft mouth and a calm eye. He carried a pennon on a pole, dark blue, a new, gleaming silk that sighed and fluttered as we rode.

To my great surprise Winter Star continued to accept the false confidence of my voice, and showed few of the high spirits of the previous day. And yet even so the horse snorted and tossed its head more than I would have wished, and I could see Sir Nigel smiling, glancing meaningfully at Wenstan.

A bet was on, I guessed. How far would it be before Winter Star bolted and left me in the mud?

Behind us rode Rannulf. His teeth gleamed through his scar. Beside Rannulf was a man I had never seen before this morning—Miles, a rotund squire, older than a knight's assistant is usually expected to be, with a charge of white through his red hair.

Miles was always singing, whistling, humming. Both Wenstan and Miles carried their master's fighting gear, a helmet, shield, and war lance. Rannulf and Nigel wore sea-blue tunics, with a blazing white Crusader star.

Even a few of the Exchequer's men smiled as we passed, and I have never been more proud or joyful than I felt that morning. As we left the city, passing Sir Nigel's hall, I felt more than happy—I felt pure at heart, cleansed of every dark thought, and every misdeed. Peasants in the field stood up from their work and saluted, their voices lost in the morning air. Sir Nigel raised a gloved hand, and so did Hubert.

And so did I.

The town dogs followed us into the farmland, a handful of them, yipping. As the highway grew long, well into the morning, they ran silently, tongues distended. This sight both heartened and saddened me, and I felt sorry for the dogs, who expected we were falconing or, at very least, heading forth to flush rabbits from their holes.

One by one the town curs dropped away, gazing after us with regret, until only a demi-hound I had seen around the kitchen middens kept our pace. The dog fell in stride with Winter Star, and the stallion shied.

"Easy," I said, and the horse shook his bridle but kept trotting.

The dog was too small to guard a hall, too big to hunt mice. Who was I to tell the animal he was making a mistake? Perhaps beasts have their Crusades, and their Heaven, too.

Shortly after midday it began to rain. Knights and men donned thick woolen cloaks with deep hoods, and the rain beaded on the wool. Winter Star splashed and curvetted in the puddles that soon appeared in the road. The high way was far from empty, huddling figures of merchants with hired guards hurrying through the rain on foot, wagoners bawling curses at their oxen, minstrels and mountebanks trudging along together.

I did not fall off my mount. But it took all my concentration, the horse inflating himself and sneezing, capering and kicking. I was exhausted by morning's end. The rain ceased in time for a midafternoon meal, the prime dinner of the day for a man of Nigel's rank. Nigel offered our Lord thanks, in our unworthiness, for this sustenance, and we ate waybread, brown, moist slices, and dry cheese made from mare's milk.

I was a little surprised that, only a few hours out of town, we were already military in provision and manner, even Hubert accepting a cup of wine from Wenstan with what he must have thought was a manly nod of the head. The dog accepted a morsel of cheese from my fingers, and Hubert gave him a healthy chunk of salted beef.

As we continued south, perhaps an hour before sunset, two great brown mastiffs rushed through the brambles on the verge of the road, and seized our dog companion by the flank and throat. Within a moment our hound was ripped in two, blood flying, the two attacking monsters gobbling and growling as they tore our dog to pieces.

Nigel whipped out his broadsword, leaned out of his saddle and sliced off a mastiff's head. Rannulf accepted his lance from Miles, balanced it, squared his shoulders, and ran down the second offending dog. The lance skewered the brute's haunch, and the great mastiff hung on the point of the lance as Rannulf lifted the kicking body clear of the road, shook his weapon, and let the body fall.

Field men ran calling out, armed with ax and staff, but when they saw the Crusader star and Rannulf's lance they fell silent.

Nigel and Wenstan headed along the high way again, Nigel without a second glance at what had happened. The knight gossiped about whose maidenhead had been lost under what hayloft. He said that a poacher had been hanged by this oak up ahead, for stealing a flitch of venison, already dressed. Or perhaps not that oak, he said, but another similar tree, back a mile or so.

I let Winter Star pace more slowly, so I might overhear what Rannulf and his man were saying. To my delight, the horse obeyed my touch at once.

"Balance, my lord," I heard Miles say. *Balaunce.* "Of course, in the case of a man, unhorsing is all that matters. Knock him, nick him."

Rannulf spoke at last. "Still, it was a pity the point was so wide of the heart."

Before we drifted to sleep, Hubert whispered from his pallet, "Did you see how angry Rannulf was, when he saw those dragons hurting our dog?"

I considered this. "He acted with due haste," I said.

"So if you or I were attacked, he would come to our aid," said Hubert.

I said that this was undoubtedly true. But privately I was not certain. I could easily imagine Rannulf watching bears consume either one of us, out of interest in the way the beasts used their claws.

When I closed my eyes I saw my master's hand, spiked to the anvil. I saw the startled eyes of our dog companion, and the spreading blood of the suddenly headless mastiff.

They say that a lion sleeps with his eyes open. Despite my fatigue, Saint Mark sent me watchfulness that night, and I kept waking to hear the slow, steady breathing of my companions.

The next morning I could scarcely stand, crippled by a day of riding, and my injured foot was aching again. I hid my discomfort, although Sir Nigel rode beside me later that morning, and said, "I've known fighting men to start the day with three flagons of the strongest cider, to ease the road-ache."

"They have my pity, my lord," I said.

Sir Nigel gave a laugh. "I bet a Flemish penny you would fall off yesterday. Rannulf collected on the wager last night."

Sometimes, even armed as we were, we traveled in a tight phalanx, Nigel at the point, sometimes standing upright in his stirrups as he rode, his gaze sweeping the forest. At times like this I dared not meet Hubert's eye, but I could sense him, tense, one hand on the pommel of his sword.

Even knights were sometimes attacked by the bandits and madmen who lived in the woods.

chapter
TEN

Innkeeper and ferryman alike greeted us with forced smiles and hollow heartiness.

Crusaders often slept in inns and forded rivers without lightening their purses, since their quest was sacred, and even the burliest wine seller had no means to enforce his fee. But Nigel paid with pennies, quartered and halved after the custom of our countryside, and the metal was always the soundest quality. Maiden and matron poured us all an extra measure of beer, and kept the tapers burning until the last of us had lurched off to our pallet in the warmest corner of the inn.

If I could be my lady's hound, no hare could hide.

Day by day, we heard all the verses of this lay as Miles sang them. We traveled south. Rain fell, the sun broke through, the wind was cold, then swung from the west and blew warm, sometimes all within an afternoon. Rivers overflowed their banks in places, and a fire had erased the shambles, the butcher's district, in one town we passed through, aproned men standing disconsolate, the smell of charred beef in the air.

Far from needing encouragement from me, it was Hubert who delighted at the sight of a flock of sheep fording a river, swimming like a vast, tufted rug. He was the one who brought a smile from the ferryman, and when he bid a mason good morning, the broad, swarthy man, powdered with sandstone, told us all that the shire bridge had been washed away, but that the ford not four miles east was no deeper than a laugh.

As we approached London the road grew populated with castle stewards and wine merchants, barrels of wine rumbling over the wagon tracks in the road, and barrels of money, too, under guard, spearmen and ox handlers alike wearing black Exchequer's armor. Oxen and dray horses labored shoulder to shoulder, wheels sending forth scythes of mud as the drovers lashed the straining beasts.

Sometimes we would pass a lady with her attendants, side-saddle, as her gentle horse picked its way through the mountains of mud, but for the most part this was a world of men, figures clotted with black mud and chalk clay, gray loam and black topsoil. God's universe was suffering a second Flood, and was transformed to mud.

"More mire," was all Hubert would say as we struggled to a hill crest and gazed at the rain-bronzed acres ahead. Priest and dairymaid climbed stiles, slathered with muck, hesitated, and descended to the mire, slogging through the deep, wet world.

In my heart I was alive with excitement, each starling's chuckle an adventure to me. I was far from the place I knew, so far that I was in a foreign land already, although we were still in England. I affected the manner of a war-wise traveler, but inside I was ablaze with curiosity.

Waking each morning was less painful to my frame now, and climbing into the saddle each time hurt less and less. After a few days I did have trouble recalling any field that was not so sodden it mirrored sky—dry dirt was distant memory. But this was a further sign that I was embarked on a high adventure. My clothes were so damp they chafed my skin, but I didn't mind. A few mornings I drank deep of Nigel's wine, and by the time we hurried toward the thatch and timber of London, knight and man among us were indistinguishable because of the skin-deep dirt.

The first *carta mundi* I had ever seen was rolled out on my master Otto's counting table, a king's clerk showing off a prize purchase, a map of the world, as rare as a mermaid's tooth. On this map London was a stand of spires and flags on a hill overlooking all of England, which lay around it in an irregular but pleasing shape, like a pie. London was at the center of the kingdom of England, and all that was beyond the pie's crust was mapmaker's fancy, a ship like a beetle, and off to one side a sea dragon with a head like a hen.

And so the real, actual city was at first a little bit of a disappointment.

At a distance in the morning sun, the great city looked like any other town that had grown beyond its walls. A smelter, or an alchemist, was melting some light metal—tin, I thought by the smell, and a walker trod around and around, treading his master's chalky earth into a powder that could be oven-fired into mortar. A wheelwright rolled one of his wares ahead of us, splashing in the gutter down the middle of the street, but it was only as we entered the town, and continued to enter it, in the shadows of the high, thatched roofs, that I was able to believe I was really in London at last.

"A mighty town!" breathed Hubert. *A mickle toun.*

Full of people speaking a tongue I scarcely understood, wearing hats of a fashion new to me, full and floppy, dyed rich colors, beet black, carrot gold. A great town that was noisy, and rich with

smells. Infants wailed, and pleasure women sang. The smell of or-
dure and incense flavored each breath. And we all fell silent as we
passed the one-hundred-year-old Conqueror's tower, where, leg-
end had it, the wall mortar had been mixed with the blood of
bears.

Indeed, I felt some shame at my road-grime. The grand streets
teemed with the king's subjects bargaining for viands in market
stalls. Fowl of all descriptions, squabs, capons, drakes, and mud
hens hung plucked and roasted. Among wine shops along the
river we jostled franklins and beggars; beyond the roofs we heard
the sounds of the river man's call.

Nigel kept to horseback, so all could see he was a knight-at-
arms and let us by unhindered, although at times Hubert called
out, "Crusading men, let us pass!"

What was missing from the populace, I thought, was the casual presence of armed men, knights and their squires, lords and
their attendants. All men of mettle had left for the Crusade, except for the few like us who hurried to join them. And some of
the men who remained looked at us from the shadows of tavern
eaves with neither smile nor shame, leaning on their staffs.

Nigel did not have to bargain long with the landlord of the
inn we reached at last, and the washerwomen he hired were waiting for us, by luck or prearrangement.

I expected Nigel to throw himself exhausted on a bunk, but
he was off at once with Wenstan, stopping me on the stair to say,
"An outward tide's at dawn!" as though this was both good and
meaningful news.

Hubert and I hurried to thrust on dry clothing and dash out
into the street. I went without arms, only a belt around my waist,
but Hubert wore his sword, a weapon that often came close to
tripping him. We shouldered past women with baskets of oysters

and great fish and small. Boys only a few years younger than ourselves tossed a ball, and scurried to retrieve it among the groaning wheels of carts. Every human creature I saw seemed alive with the thrill of living in this town, except for those tall, unsmiling men I had remarked before, armed with hand-pike or quarterstaff, eyeing women as they bustled past.

Over all the streets hung an odor, not human or animal, not wood smoke, a taste of river, huge and deep, like the flavor of a whelk on the tongue.

And the river spread before us at last, dotted with gigs and skiffs, the small craft the river men use for harvesting shellfish. There were other boats on it, too, sea-stained ships pulling up the river with the help of long sweeps, wooden oars that gave the ships the look of waterbugs gliding on long legs. We climbed down the bank and waded in the current, river mud tickling through our toes.

On the way back to the inn, a dray horse stood, head hanging in the street. A burly man with a bald head wielded a quarterstaff, striking the horse on its broad back. Each blow sent a shiver down the animal's flesh, but the horse took a long, rib-expanding breath, and let it out, enduring. I had seen many such beatings in my life, and so, no doubt, had Hubert.

But something about the bald man's grin of concentration as he belabored the horse stiffened Hubert.

Hubert told the man to cease.

The bald man did stop, but only to stand with an exaggerated stance of incomprehension. *"Ceese!"* he echoed, mocking Hubert's voice.

I stepped before the man, and put a hand lightly on his chest.

"Take your friend the pup and lose yourself," he said, smelling of beer and sweat. It took me a moment to make sense of what he said.

To punctuate our conversation, he lifted the staff and struck the horse on the back so hard the horse shuddered, and only a quick lurch of its hindquarters kept it from falling. A small throng had gathered, grinning, nudging, but most of the citizens had places to go, and I tried to restrain Hubert by saying, jokingly, "This man will be tired soon."

"Take his staff from him, and break it," said Hubert.

But the man understood enough of our English to level his staff at me, feint, and thrust it hard into my belly.

I gasped, not badly hurt, but certainly surprised. I was slow in grabbing at the staff, because the drover danced away from me, like a wrestler at a summer fair. He braced himself, staff held across his body in the way of peasants when they fight.

"Leave be, leave be," said a short, bent man. He coughed, the dry hack of a fuller, one of those laborers who knead starch and salts into wool. Such men breathe years of sheep-chaff, and their insides grow soft and furry.

"We just delivered some two hundred ells of wool bound for Flanders," said the fuller. "And happy to have it off our hands, we stop by for a sip of drink, and now the horse decides he has a willful nature." This, at least, was what I understood him to be saying.

"We're crusading squires from Nottingham," I said, keeping my answer short, because the bald man was brandishing the staff and rising to his toes, shifting one way and another, staring at Hubert like the champion man-and-dray-horse beater of London, no challenger declined.

Hubert's sword was a flash, just as the staff whipped downward. A sharp, heart-stopping crack, and the drover's staff was cut in two.

I expected Hubert to be astonished at what I took to be a fluke, slicing a quarterstaff as thick as his arm. But Hubert moved quickly, tripped the man, put one foot in the drover's chest, and the point of the broadsword at his throat.

"Don't kill him!" cried the fuller. "He's got a new wife and a new little baby—"

This was no common weapon, the blade in Hubert's hand. The length and span of it reflected roof peaks and the sky. Hubert did not acknowledge the sound of my voice until I tugged his sleeve, like a man in jest, and said, "Let him live just this once, good Hubert."

I put my arm around the fuller, and said that if he applied at the White Hart inn my lord, Sir Nigel, would pay for the staff, and reward the fuller's patience for not seeking the attention of a magistrate. The fuller might have worked out a retort to this, but he bent over, hands on his knees, racked with coughing.

I took Hubert by the arm. I dragged him stumbling and protesting, down along the dockside, among coils of brown rope and barrels of wine. One or two of the barrels had sprung leaks, or had been purposefully gimletted so a sneak thief could suck his fill. Rats scampered among purple puddles and a customs man in a red cloak called to us, "Out, out," without rising from his stool.

We could not find the way.

As I straddled the gutter trickling down the center of the street, I was tall enough to see over the heads and shoulders of the

56

passing Londoners. We walked without talking, until we stood at the edge of a broad field.

A reeve sat on a swaybacked horse, nodding and gesturing to two peasants. Rooks filled a leaf-bare chestnut tree, and the road ahead was a footpath.

We retraced out steps, and walked purposefully, looking neither to the right nor the left, past a tavern of pleasure women with more clothes around their hips and ankles, all swirls and ribbons, than on their chests and shoulders. We marched all the way to a flat deserted place, timber piled pink and fresh among weeds, keels set up on wooden braces. A shirtless man in the warm late afternoon sun plied an adze, white curls of wood falling to the ground.

"We've lost our way just a bit, good boatwright," I said. "Could you please direct us to—"

The man shook his head and uttered something in a language more obscure and guttural than any I had ever heard.

He laughed at our crestfallen expression, not unkindly, a man red and gold from sun. "No English," he said, as though the thought of speaking like one of us gave him wholehearted amusement. "Norge," he said, touching his chest with his thumb. "Norwayan. Ha!"

We were lost.

chapter
ELEVEN

Hubert told Sir Nigel everything we had done when we returned, after many winding alleys, to the inn.

"It is really a blessing that we arrived when we did," concluded Hubert, "to help the horse in its distress."

Sir Nigel set his wine cup down and looked into it as though a toad peered up at him from the interior.

"But it's all right now, my lord," added Hubert. "And I doubt that the horse will be beaten any time again soon."

Sir Nigel looked at Hubert without any expression on his face, and then he looked at me.

I opened my mouth, but just as quickly I shut it again. The oak beams in the ceiling creaked.

"I can't blame you, Hubert," Nigel said, "for nearly slaughtering a drover on your first afternoon in London. After all, you had an idle hour, why not kill a man?"

Hubert and I did not speak.

"We'll be leaving before dawn tomorrow," Nigel said. "and in your absence the inn has taken on more travelers that it can hold. But there's a perfectly good place for you to sleep."

Wenstan led us down toward the river, and out along a planked wharf. It was early evening, and the smell of frying fish mingled with the carrion-stench of a tannery. Wenstan clambered up a rope ladder and looked back, expectantly.

I hesitated.

I had never been on a ship before, nor any boat—not even so much as a floating log.

Wenstan beckoned.

A spiderweb of rigging swept upward into the dark. The rope ladder was knotted and spliced, and I slipped and fumbled my way up, and onto the deck. Even in this slack river current the ship rose and fell creaking under our feet. Hubert gazed at the mast and rigging wide-eyed, and I put out a hand to steady myself, clinging to a rope that stretched across the growing dark.

An explosion of furious language met me, and I released the rope. A sailor hurried from some perch in the ship's upper recesses and tested the rope I had deigned to set my hand upon. He gave it a tug, observing its effect on the mast. The sailor continued to scold, a stream of words more foreign to me than any London chatter.

Hubert and I crept down a short wooden ladder, and peered into a dark space, so shallow a dog could not have stood on his four legs.

"This is wonderful!" said Hubert, excitedly. "I knew Sir Nigel would find us a noble ship!"

The ship rose on the river current, stayed up for a long time, so long it was easy to forget it had ever ascended. And then it descended, down, all the way down into some nerve-chilling abyss in the river. The ship drew away from the dock, and halted with a jolt when it reached the extent of its mooring. It swung sideways, and dug hard against the wharf.

The boat's uneasiness could not continue, I thought, and must be the result of some temporary disturbance in the river. But as the ship shied and shook, timbers grunting, I began to feel the stirrings of a sensation very much like fear.

People did not look upon hills and mountains as anything but waste, dangerous and without light, a domain of the thousand-year-old spirits who were anything but human. The sea was even worse. It was an abyss, a void that no man looked upon with joy except for those unlucky enough to be sailors.

I was cold, and I felt the stirrings of nausea. The ship shuddered out from under me and rose to take me up again. People went forth on ships to die.

I did not sleep.

chapter
TWELVE

Our ship nosed out into the river while a mist was thin on the water, the sun just rising.

The river was crowded along the banks with laystalls, latrines that emptied into the lapping water. Dung boats poured their still-steaming loads into the current, the scent of human soil lost in the odor of fires and the rising vapor of ditches that emptied into the current. Other ships were rolling out into the river, too, and in the cold vapor of morning the ships sounded horns, like hunters, the brassy notes mingling with the sound of birds on either bank.

I kept glancing in Rannulf's direction, but the knight was hidden in a dark robe and cowl. Only two long oars were needed to propel the ship forward, following the tide toward the open sea, and the sailors who manned the oars rowed with spirit, calling to each other with an easygoing cheer.

The horses were lashed together, and hobbled with rawhide tethers. Shadow, Hubert's mount, was as gentle as a maiden, and all the other horses, including Nigel's and Rannulf's stout chargers, accepted shipboard life with some degree of patience. Winter Star was the only animal that required a blindfold before he would stop whinnying and plunging, and even then he was quiet only when I stood beside him and spoke in a gentle voice.

I told him that all was well, and I told him that our ship was manned with seamen of the most skilled variety. I rattled on and on, and as long as I kept talking Winter Star was erect, like the statue of a horse, except that now and then he had to put forth a hoof to check his balance.

As soon as I left his side, and crept to the bucket, and poured a scoop of fresh water over my head, Winter Star would snort. Shivers ran up and down under his skin, his muscles twitching.

"Are you well?" asked Sir Nigel.

"I have never felt better," I answered, because grumbling is the Devil's Paternoster. "How long, my lord, before we see land again?"

"I do believe we're still on the river, Edmund," he said.

"Of course, my lord. I meant—when we set forth on the sea—"

"It's been known to take a month to cross the channel," he said.

A month of this!

"But God willing not so long for us," said Sir Nigel with a laugh.

"A channel, my lord," I had to ask, "between what land and what other land?"

But he seemed to not hear me. I thought he looked pale, himself, and he took only a sip of Crete-wine and water, when Wenstan offered it. Nigel joined Rannulf, the two of them standing, hooded like priests.

Hubert was everywhere, upside down to watch the foam flow, halfway up the mast to see a gull diving time and again in the water, cheering when the bird flew off, a fish living gold in its beak.

By daylight I was hanging my head over the side of the ship, staring down into the my own shadow. I vomited several times, like a sneeze, emptying what little I had in my belly into the eddies of the ship's wake. And after that I emptied nothing, and vomited with the pointlessness of a dog who will not stop barking.

I prayed in my weakness, not unlike the offering of a dying man to Heaven. I begged the aid of Our Lord Jesu, from whom proceeds all understanding and goodness. I wished for a rosary, with its gaudy beads, but instead closed my eyes and opened my heart to Heaven.

Holy mass is not celebrated on board any ship, as a rule, lest an errant wave or a cursing sailor violate the worship. But I would have benefited from some divine solace that day. The smell of breakfast cheese froze me, wrenched my innards, and, I am afraid, made my skin turn the very color of death.

The air changed. The light brightened, the haze turning the color of egg white. No one moved.

The sailors hushed. Nigel and Rannulf looked upward.

With a flutter of soft thunder a sail fell open, shrugged and struggled like a living thing, and bellied out with wind.

Alive, the ship coursed, the spray freshening our faces. Hubert leaned as far out as he could, and Miles sang a song about kissing his lady's bed with his keel. The wind did much to clear the fog, but a fine rain began to fall, and this gray low cloud stayed just close enough to keep us from seeing landmarks, as though the sky were a huge tent that we traveled within.

But eventually even an ignorant landsman like myself could tell that the ship was soaring skyward one moment and falling down into the trough the next, and I did not have to be told that we had left the river.

The Book of the Lion

We had reached the channel, and every misery I had suffered was now multiplied. Winter Star was reeling, trying to rear up, and as carefree as the sailors were, they stayed well away from the stallion's hooves. I crawled back to my place at Winter Star's side, and with a bow and a smile a sailor provided me with a four-legged stool. The seaman gave me a long, kind-hearted, utterly foreign discourse on the nature of sea and wind.

Rannulf and Nigel stood silent, faces hidden in the dark hoods, but Wenstan spoke with the helmsman, a grinning, bearded fellow, who from time to time would lever the tiller out of the water and look back at it, water dripping off the broad steering oar. Sometimes a crook of seaweed was tangled there, and the helmsman would shake it free.

"Who are these men?" I asked Sir Nigel, declining a taste from his goatskin of wine.

"These are Cornishmen," said Nigel.

"Are they taking us all the way to Jerusalem?" I asked. I knew that the Holy City was so far away that people who journeyed there returned, if they came home at all, white-haired and wasted.

Nigel chuckled. "They are taking us to Normandy."

This news meant very little to me. The second, and finest, map of the world I had ever studied had been spread out on Father Joseph's table. I had stopped by that afternoon to deliver a just-repaired chalice. Father Joseph saw the look in my eye, and explained, saying, "This is a true map of Earth under Heaven."

"Where is London?" I had asked.

As usual, Father Joseph punctuated his speech with a belch. Most men I know are troubled with wind, being fond of windy foods, cabbage and red meat. He said, "London is an unimportant place, Edmund, a speck of stone and humanity, compared with the Holy City."

64

All of England was a little crumb off to the west of a mighty hill. On the summit stood a castle, with towers from which grew fruit trees. "Jerusalem," explained Father Joseph reverently, "is the center of the world."

Perhaps it was the sin of envy I experienced, watching Hubert rabbiting from stem to stern. Envy is sorrow at the prosperity of others, and Hubert prospered in his great health. But I did not wish him sorrow, and took no joy when he slipped on the wet deck and had to sit down for a while, blinking thoughtfully at the small rain that drifted down.

Just when I thought I could not endure another moment, the lookout gave a cry.

The actual words meant little to me, but I understood.

"Land," I whispered to Winter Star. The horse pricked up his ears, shook his head. "So soon!"

But it was merely a scow awash with flounders, so full of the silver-bright, still-flapping fish, that the squat vessel could not swing out of our way. Long poles were used to fend off the fishing boat.

My first sight of Normandy was the following dawn.

When the ridge of white sand appeared above the leaden water I took little notice, fearing another disappointment. But Winter Star snorted at the scent of fields, and the sailors worked the sweeps, the long oars, out through the oarlocks, and shortened the sail.

I did not want to give myself over to happiness. Not yet.

At last I saw footprints stitching the beach, clear, definite shapes, and saw a fisherman spreading his net. A peasant stood in the sunlight and emptied his bladder, an amber arc of blessed human piss.

chapter
THIRTEEN

We sat around a table at an inn and the landlord served a platter of young lamb, gold roasted, plaice in jelly, and stewed figs made with honey and cinnamon. A carver served out the food, ladled it onto trenchers of wheat bread. One taste of lamb brought tears to my eyes.

A riverman had spied a ghost, a woman who had been raped and cut to pieces by traveling knights. She was said to haunt the reeds along the river.

"Foolish people!" Hubert was saying. "The saints steadfastly protect a Christian from such ghosts."

"Do knights in this countryside ride about rutting and murdering?" I asked.

"Of course they do!" said Nigel. "God's lips, any knight would, except for fear of Hell. That's why the lord pope has seen the wisdom in sending so many fighting men to the Holy Land. That and, of course, the great need of us there."

"A ghost is but a demon," said Hubert. "However its disguise, I'll spit on it, even if it carries its head like a bucket."

———

But the next day, on board our new vessel, we all studiously ignored the banks of the river, lest one of the aproned, matronly figures prove to be headless. Nor did we look up when a bird slipped from tree to tree calling an unfamiliar song, *No return, no return.*

Behind hedge and cattle trough a devil might be hiding.

Wenstan and Miles disagreed on a song about a woman in a citadel who grew her hair long, so any passing knight could climb up the long tresses and join her in corporeal delight. Miles contended that the hair in question was her privy hair, while Wenstan said this was the most irritating example of twisting a jolly song into something sinful. "It was the hair of her head," stammered Wenstan. "Her head hair!"

One evening a cow swam across the river, and the rivermen slowed the ship so it wouldn't collide with the surging, lowing head. I could only wonder that the cow could have wandered so far from her usual pasture, and her companions. Now that it was feeding time the beast was near lost, and Hubert and I stood in the stern of the river ship and watched the cow for a long time, until she disappeared along the bank, her bell ringing softly in the willows.

We made our way through forest and farm when we had left the river behind.

When we found no inn, Wenstan and Miles drove tall camp pegs into the soil, long wooden spears, with a shape like a nailhead at one end, and erected a great, sail-gray tent. The thick canvas bellied and fluttered until willing hands caught the ropes and helped to tie it down.

In the midst of strange country, a bull across a stream gazing at us, a few hammer blows, a few quick knots, and the sky, the foreign landscape, was hidden by canvas. I told Wenstan how magnificent our tent was, and he said, after preparing his tongue to utter the words, "Good Edmund, when you see the tents of Our Lord's army, you'll think this dull."

I had heard of monstrous men in far-off lands, men whose faces and brains were in their chests, who had no heads, and the race of humans called unipeds, who bounded along the ground on one massive leg.

In our whispered speculation Hubert and I agreed that to meet one man-monster would be a disturbing sight, but an army of them would strike terror.

Each evening Hubert and I would practice sword work, Nigel looking on, calling, "Stance, watch your stance!" or "With a will, Edmund!" I learned how to hold my sword in the high ward, over my head, and the low ward, angled down by my knees. Nigel taught me to look at armor with a squire's eye, how to help a knight dismount with a strong and willing shoulder, and how to assist with a war lance, dusting the grip with resin powder.

Some farms had been blight-blasted and abandoned, house and granary burned to the ground. Others flourished. The vineyards sent forth yellow-green shoots, and the wheat fields were bare except for shivering, bright new life. Church bells reached us sounding oddly sour, the music of the call to prayer made bitter by our growing distance from home.

I slept well at night. We ate the hen's eggs and pullets Wenstan bargained for in nearby farms. We consumed goat and jellied eels, wine by the pottleful, sheep's milk, and pies of swan's necks and goose livers, steaming hot.

The road was long, and the river was longer, and as the days and weeks went by each one of us grew lean and brown. We rarely rode our war mounts on these long, journeying days, but kept to cobs purchased for the trip, mild animals, bred for burden, destined for the poor man's table.

Some breezy, rain-spattered days we traveled by cattle barge along a river, magpies stalking the vineyards. Other days we traveled by cart-rutted path, always waking well before dawn and settling for the night while the sun was still high in the sky.

It was clear that the gray, stooped men Wenstan bargained with for cheese and bread were afraid of us. They would not meet Hubert's eye, or mine.

"Is Saladin a monster, too?" I was asking.

"A monster?" echoed Nigel. He gave his horse an absent-minded pat, waving away a wasp. The wasp persisted, and Nigel leaned from side to side, cursing, dodging the insect.

We rode in a long line, and the horses had been nervous, their ears twitching. I shook out a sword-cloth from my pack, and snapped it at the wasp. Perhaps it was a lucky blow—the tiny creature vanished.

"You know how I hate such pests," said Nigel, gratefully.

"The pagan lord," I persisted. "Is he a terrible demon, like his men, or is he built like us, with arms, and legs, and—all the other parts?"

"The pagans we call Mussulmen. I know little about them, I am pleased to say. They have taken the Holy City from the Christians, but I am certain, Edmund, that they look in great measure as we do."

A dozen questions swarmed in me. Did these heathens fight with swords? Did they invoke the Devil, and did the Devil ride with them?

Some pigs were eating the carcass of a dray horse beside the road. Two young sows ran off at our approach, but the largest, a brown and pink matron sow stayed, snout deep in the ribs of a nearly fleshless skeleton.

Hubert threw a stone the size of a grouse egg, small and smooth, and it struck the pig squarely on its right ham. The pig did not look up, but it did argue a little, making a sound like Sir Nigel talking in his sleep.

Rannulf accepted the lance from his squire, swung it easily up and down to check the balance.

Nigel cried out, "I can smell it!"

"We all nose this poor horse, my lord," I said.

Nigel lifted his hand. "No, Edmund—I smell the sea!"

chapter
FOURTEEN

The ship was called *Sant' Agnese*.

It was a holy ship. Even coiling a rope preparing for the voyage, the sailors made the sign of the Cross, so that, as Wenstan explained, a demon could not get wound up in the circles of cordage.

"This is not a ship," breathed Hubert. "This is a castle!"

Indeed, the Cornish boat that had carried us across the channel now seemed like an oyster-catcher's wherry, compared to this floating cathedral. Dockers carried casks of honey, sacks of wheat and millet flour, bales of kidskin leather, barrels of wine from the Rhone vineyards. As the ship took on cargo, we feasted on roasted curlew, purchased under the sky, still hot from the spit. Provender for the voyage was brought in cages, ducks, thrusting necks through the wooden staves of the crates, hens squawking, and a single rooster in a cage by himself, crowing.

Dozens of men manned the sweeps, and we surged away from the dock, overlooked by an image of the blessed Saint Agnes, set upright at the prow. The beloved saint held a lamb in her arms, and looked down upon us with patient love.

———

One hour out of port the sail filled with wind and the bottom of the sea fell out from under us. The ship dropped straight down for a long time, a wall of water growing higher on all sides. The sunlight vanished, and the shade of the sea was chill.

"Be strong, Edmund!" said Hubert softly into my ear.

Not a single sailor looked upward with any concern, each seaman with some task that took all his attention, stowing ration sacks, untying or tying knots, clinging to the tiller, calmly busy.

Our captain was named Sebastiano Nero, a short, heavyset man with a bronze laugh. He folded his arms, and looked up at the sky.

The walls of water clapped together overhead, and the white, rushing suds of brine swept me off my feet. Two sailors seized me, patted my back, but another wave fell forward, and only the strong arms of the sailors kept me from floating like a cork up and over the scuppers.

Rannulf was at my side as I sprawled, soaked through. He took my arm in a steel grip. "Take this sennit rope," he said. "Tie yourself around the waist." He looped the rope and knotted it as he spoke. I felt grateful beyond words.

The ship bucked. The horses, including Winter Star, screamed. But they were in an enclosure, a timber and canvas stable just beyond the mast, and the more fearful of them lashed out with a hind hoof at anyone who tried to approach.

I was surprised when Rannulf spoke further to me. "It will profit God nothing," said the knight, "if you drown."

Seas towered, mountains that fumed and spumed before they collapsed over our heads. Sebastiano Nero barked orders and laughed. His laugh was more genuinely good-humored than Nigel's.

The sky was blue, and the sun winked and peered over the

massifs of sea, and even at sunset, when the sky was evening calm, stars standing forth out of the dark, the vessel plunged and shook so that no one but the saltiest sailor was able to walk from the stern to the prow without clutching at the man-ropes.

Rannulf and Nigel gathered dignity about them, and stayed within, in a berth packed with straw and dry, soft wool blankets. Hubert and I were stowed in a less spacious, darker quarter of the ship, and while Hubert sought to view the crashing waters from various vantage points, high and low, I sought the ship's side.

I spent hours there. I suffered what the sailors called *dolento di mare,* although others argued *dolente del oceane,* or even *dol' di mar,* until my seasickness became a cheerful point of dispute among seagoing scholars. No one could agree on what to call the *disjecta* from my belly, either, although *vomito* was the word I most easily recognized. One Genoan giant with blue trousers called out something every time I hung my head over the side, and coughed up my empty belly: The English youth is singing.

If I heaved and brought forth nothing but an agonizing belch, the Genoan would comment. If I slipped and fell down as I barked forth empty air this gave rise to comment, too.

Day by day I felt more seaworthy.

I could close my eyes without feeling that I was plummeting, and I scented fish frying on a coal brazier without convulsing. Stars swung wide and the moon joined them in a nightly dance, but the sight began to seem a pleasure to me, as did the coursing movement of the ship, only two fingers of planking between my listening ear and the quickness of the ocean.

One noontime the giant Genoan laughed as I took Wenstan's wine sack in my hands, and drank deeply. Like any man of sense, Wenstan knew that water was rich with disease of every nation, but sweet Loire wine carried no fever. I drank as much as was seemly, and thanked Wenstan. I let the giant laugh. I joined him, laughing.

I would surprise this big man.

I walked to where he stood, this giant binding the end of a rope with a yellow, bristling twine. I took the rope from his hands in a sudden gesture, and I was near to making a market loop, a dairyman's favorite, one I had seen at market day every week of my life. You tie a noose, toss it over the dumb head of your prize cow, and lead her where you will.

The Genoan said something, good-humored and challenging.

A hand pressed my elbow. "We need this sailor alive and well, Edmund," said Hubert.

"I was only going to show him how we splice a knot in England." Around a bully's head, I did not add.

"Everyone is watching," whispered Hubert.

Indeed, from every point on the ship, from tiller to Saint Agnes, sailors looked up from their work.

With a smile the Genoan took the rope from my hands, whipped the twine around the rope end, and presented it to me. He worked a small dagger from his belt, sawed briefly at the rope, and left it in my hands.

I felt myself blush, bested by his fierce good-humor.

Our last remaining chicken, the white rooster, crowed time and again. The cook had hung his cage on the mast, perhaps so his last day among the living could be a pleasure.

It was another warm day, seabirds eyeing us from above, the smell of a shore in the wind, fishnets and shellfish and cattle, although the land was far away, a brown wrinkle above the sea.

Miles was singing the song about the gander who caught his neck in milady's bower.

The lookout called from above, announcing a *barca*. There was usually an hour, or even half a day, between the lookout's cry and the actual approach of a ship full of silks or cloves, lumbering heavy laden from the fabled east.

But this time I caught the scent, man-sweat and wet timber, within minutes. I stood in time to watch Hubert climb the rigging. Rannulf stepped from the shade and spat over the side of the ship, into the sea. The sailors made a show of demonstrating no great interest in this floating building that bore down on us, two great brass-tipped horns protruding from its prow.

But none of us spoke, unless to put on an affection of ease, the Genoan taking a commanding interest in lashing a sweep to a pin.

Our Venetian captain sent a man to the mast to shake down a blue-and-white Crusader banner, but even so the galley backed oars and came around. A line of turbaned, bearded men gazed down at us, with a show of smiles. The cloths on their heads were brilliant colors, a dyer's pride, plum scarlet, peacock blue. The swords at their hips were crescents, like the early moon, and the sun flashed from the steel.

The oars on the far side of the ship splashed, and the shadow of the galley darkened our deck and took the gentle wind from our sails.

"Infidels," said Nigel, in a low voice. He made the sign of the cross. "Not a single man of them a Christian."

I did not have the habit, as most men-at-arms did, of keeping my broadsword where I could quickly fasten it around my waist. I stood naked of arms, and felt cold.

"They will board us," I said, in a husky voice.

"*A Venezia,*" cried Sebastiano in answer to a question. I had never heard him use this taut, courteous tone before.

A turbaned man leaned over the side of the galley, his shadow falling over us. He was dressed in trousers, fluttering sea-blue silk, and had a wide belt with a buckle of bronze. He stretched an arm.

"*Cavaliere,*" cried our captain, hitching his belt. "*Inglese.*"

Two or three of the men in dazzling turbans gestured, and their own captain chuckled.

"They admire the redness of your hair," Sir Nigel told Miles. "Like sunrise. Or a sunset."

"Do you speak Mussulman, my lord?" asked Miles in a raspy voice.

"They are speaking a sort of Venetian, which anyone can understand. Look—they are admiring you, Edmund," said Nigel. "They say you look every inch a fighting man."

chapter
FIFTEEN

"Why didn't they board and kill us all?" I asked.

"They wouldn't want to wet their swords with the likes of us." Sir Nigel laughed. "That ship was out of Constantinople. Those men are friendly to the Venetians, and sometimes help Christians reach the Holy Land."

"They betray their own Infidel brothers?" I asked.

"It is strange," admitted Nigel. "There is no understanding what men raised under the sun will do. Perhaps heat makes them all half mad."

A sailor kneeling in the prow dropped a sink line, and called out, *"quat' bracci."* The line made a whisper as it was reeled in. After a short silence, the plumb-knob splashed and the line sank again.

Every time the cry was nearly the same—four fathoms, or three.

Nigel and Rannulf ate the rooster, roasted on a spit, while the rest of us ate the first salt meat we had tasted on this voyage. It was a pink-fleshed smoke-flavored pork the sailors ate with relish. I thought it a good dish, but tar-flavored, like wine that has been stored in greenwood barrels.

Our ship bumped some submerged object, a floating cask or log. In recent hours we had encountered much debris, charred beef bones, hen coops, tun-staves. But this was an unusually large drift-bole, and it bumped and gently battered the keel as we sailed on over it, and bobbed up in our moonlit wake.

From afar Venice was like an army of pitched tents and glorious pennons in the late sun, floating on smoke.

We could not approach the waters of the city itself, because the sea was crowded with warships and pinnaces, rowboats, fisher-boats, boats appointed with gold and thick dark carpets, and salt-stained barges. Some of the ships were heavy in the water, and gave off the perfumes of peppercorn and clove, guarded by men in red or yellow trousers, carrying spears with brilliant crescent-moon blades.

"Not one of those spearmen is worth a serf's wage," said Rannulf.

I was surprised and flattered at his quiet word, leaning with me over the glittering surface of the tide. "They look dangerous to me," I allowed.

"Looking dangerous is everything to the warriors of the East," said Rannulf.

I couldn't keep myself from asking. "What would your plan of attack be, in a fight with one of those spearmen?"

Rannulf's scarred lips twisted into a smile. "What would you recommend, Edmund?"

I could not meet his gaze for a moment, aware that this was more than an idle question. "I'd let the spearman make the first move, seize the shaft, and try to take it away from him."

He shook with silent humor.

"I'd take the spear in my hands," I insisted, "and break it over my knee."

He laughed aloud, and I felt rebuffed.

"I don't mock you, Edmund," said Rannulf. "I hope to see you break many a heathen spear, and before too many weeks."

Nigel returned from a brief visit on the docks. He spent a moment huddling with Rannulf and Wenstan. Hubert perched in the rigging, and when the meeting broke up he bounded along the deck to my place beside the horse enclosure.

"The fighting is already underway!" said Hubert. "Christians and Mussulmen have begun fighting in the Holy Land!"

I was bitter with disappointment at this news. I was gathering up the leather feed bags, the horses having eaten, and placing the bags in a leather-hinged trunk.

"The Christian knights are laying siege to the great castle-town of Acre," said Hubert. "But King Richard is not yet there."

You are too late, the gulls sang.

Too late, too late.

chapter
SIXTEEN

Morning was hot.

The sea gave off an odor like shellfish soup, the sailors sweating heavily. The gray, weather-mottled sails were furled, oars drawn up, and there was nothing to do but wait for the customs officials to climb aboard.

Venice was a riot of red plumes and brass pier-knobs, gold flags and messengers in purple stockings. All of it beyond reach. A squealing, spinning music from above descended upon us. Swallows, small, dark birds, spiraled and lofted into the sky.

Hurry, their cries said to my ears. *The Crusade is almost done.*

We paced, impatient, as the long day grew hotter. Hubert convinced me that Richard was tarrying in Sicily, on the Greek islands. We would reach Acre before the king, and surely the fighting would not end before Richard drew sword.

When the official vessel, a sleek, black oar-driven craft, reached our ship, the men did not board at once. Even though this was a ship of Italian sailors, there was something wrong with our captain's papers, the red seals and the yellow ribbons on the documents the wrong color, or illegible. Sebastiano laughed angrily, swept his arm at the sky, at the sea, at all of our expectant faces.

A black kidskin sack was pressed into the hand of one of the men in the boat, with a show of apology, and a gesture of *Sant' Agnese* in the prow.

Each official gave the sack a toss, opened it, peered within. They looked around at the green harbor water, and the hundreds of ships, each waiting for a customs visit. A shrug. A long discussion about documents and Englishmen, knights and fools. There was no hurry—we could all stay like this while the Crusade was fought out to a conclusion far, far away.

All aboard the *Sant' Agnese* had to stand in a line while a Venetian surgeon's apprentice examined our gums and the whites of our eyes, as though we were nanny goats at a market.

Sebastiano kept up a running commentary, how brave we were, that Acre was under siege, time was running through our fingers. The head customs official reminded me of Alan, the Exchequer's man. The pale Venetian stood, one hand on his hip, looking me up and down, and made a joke to one of his companions. They chuckled, added a quip of their own, and there was much laughter.

"What are they saying?" I asked.

"Something lewd, I fear, Edmund," and Sir Nigel with good humor. "This is a city of great vice."

The city is a rambling, sea-moss-encrusted place, surrounded on all sides by water. I had never seen a more dismal town.

If a man chose to walk off down one street to exercise his legs, he soon came to the end of the city, and stood at the edge of nothing but salt water. After so long aboard ship, I needed soil, and trees, and fields, and all I could find was bustling marketplace, and steps leading up, steps leading down, canals and water all around.

"Somewhere in the city," said Hubert, "are the bones of Saint Mark."

For some time I had the fervent hope that I could worship before these relics. But I lost my way. The marketplace was full of bins of yellow fruit called *limones*, a fruit smaller that a hen's egg, with a thick yellow skin and large, uneven pores, like a tanner's nose. One bite of the flesh of this fruit brings tears to the eyes. Caged yellow birds sang, the sweetest music I had ever heard, and the small birds pecked crumbs when I poked my fingers through the bars of their prisons. The bread for sale was white, with a good brown crust, but full of empty gaps and bubbles.

Fine ale was not to be had, unless in the taverns where Bremen town sailors sat and sang songs no one else knew. Wine they had, sound wine, unmixed with water, and other, inferior vintages polluted with herbs. Many times I had seen wine merchants pilloried in my boyhood, for selling wine doctored with gum and resin. Here the Tuscan red wine was adulterated without fear of punishment. Women could be rented by the hour in the inns overlooking the large canal. The women I saw were like plucked chickens, all flesh and breast, with paint on their cheeks and around their eyes.

Not that I took displeasure in the sight of them. I did envy Nigel when I saw the knight with two such companions, making way up a stone staircase. Rannulf perched in a corner of the tavern, tossing a pair of dice in his hand. He was listening to a squat, merry man in russet stockings. Miles sat beside him, his face flushed, his eyes gleaming.

Rannulf listened to the man in russet stockings, turned to ask

Miles something. Miles did not have to respond. Rannulf reached across the table, and popped the two dice into the jolly fellow's mouth. Rannulf and his squire stood and left the tavern, looking with an indifferent glance up and down the canal, before marching back in the direction of the ship. Miles was a bright-colored shadow, almost too cheerful to be the companion to such a lean, dark-eyed man.

I felt a stab of envy, that most powerful of sins. Miles shared Rannulf's insights and his moods, as I could not. And as I watched Rannulf straightened with a quiet laugh at something Miles had said.

"Have you ever played a dicing game?" asked Hubert, as the man with the russet stockings grinned at us through the window, giving his moist dice a toss.

The gambler stepped into the street, welcoming us, good Englishmen, travelers from the far sea. Or so I caught his meaning. He would play for no money at all. He was just learning his trade, a fledgling gambler. *He* would pay *us,* if we would but come inside.

Hubert and I found another wine shop, on another street. We bought two great goatskin sacks of red wine, sacks with the legs still sticking out. Each mouthful of wine tickled the tongue with a few more hairs of the billygoat, but the wine was dark and unnaturally sweet, seeping through the sack seams like tar.

When we had drunk our fill of this liquor, we flung the empty goatskins into the canal, and pissed upon them, *Heh, heh, heh,* cried Hubert, an excellent imitation of Captain Sebastiano. We found a tavern with a monkey in a golden cage, and a dog trained to walk on its hind legs, and watched as the small animal obediently and with eager eyes, stepped lightly from table to table, accepting morsels and applause. By then we had tasted some of the tavern's negus, a warm, spice-flavored cup I drank straight off and called for another.

Hubert stood and declared for all to hear, "This dog is a slave to our amusement," a remark that caused great laughter.

Hubert climbed onto a chair. "While brave men and godly men are dying outside Acre, we are bedeviled!"

Again, great cheer.

But when Hubert gathered the small, white-fleeced dog into his arms, the outcry was deafening. Even out on the narrow street the crowd of shouting men flowed after us, the bright eyes of the dog peering from Hubert's arms.

The night was warm, and lanterns pierced the dark from windows high above. The city was a poor place for a flight or fight. Cornered under a window with red curtains, Hubert held the dog to his chest, like a babe in arms, and he called, "Get me my sword, Edmund!"

His sword, and mine, were aboard the *Sant'Agnese,* and we had no defense but my two fists. I called for Hubert, but the thick air slowed my voice, deafened us all. I felt no fear. Something about the thick, humid evening made me feel that I could explain Hubert's character in eloquent Venetian.

Before I could swing my fists, the throng had us.

We were dumped into the canal, and by the same hands, pulled out again, patted and caressed, and guided back to the tavern. Laughter, hearty voices. I spat a mouthful of water that tasted like over-salty parsnip soup. Like most people, I could not swim, and a plunge in water gave me no pleasure.

The dog yipped, and walked on his hind legs, beseeching our attention, but the tavern keeper threw a market hitch over its neck, and led the pet away.

Hubert and I sat dripping onto the floor, the water that pattered from our clothing gleaming in the candlelight. The innkeeper plied us with warm cups of spiced wine, rolls of cinnamon and tiny wooden stars of cloves floating at the bottom of each cup, a summer's-wages worth of spices.

What an odd sound laughter is! To make it we bare our teeth, and howl like hounds. We sat near a fire of apple wood and balsam, a sweet scented heat that dried our clothes. Hubert danced with a woman of great size. His feet were nimble, to no particular pattern of the lyre tune. The monkey was released from his cage, and climbed up Hubert's head and shoulders, as a man might shinny up a pier in rising water. I joined in the great general laughter.

Later, as we were once again carried into out the darkness, and hurled into a dank mossy corner, my mouth was still paralyzed in a puzzled smile. Not for the first time, I doubted the amusement of the evening, and tried to call out to Hubert.

Hands searched me, for what little silver I had left, found it, took it away. I called for Hubert again, and heard him sigh, and sigh again, as a leather clad foot kicked him, rhythmically and with continuing intensity. Our attackers were laughing.

As I clambered to my feet, I puzzled over what word Hubert had spoken, what proverb he had recited, that gave particular amusement to these violent men.

The other assailants wearied, but a stout man with a black, plush cloak did not abate his fierce attack on Hubert, except, after a while, to alter feet, and kick all the harder with his left foot. *Come away,* the cloaked man's companions called in their own bird-lively tongue.

Or words that carried the same meaning. I could not blame

them for regarding us as figures of entertainment, and for finding that the sport was pretty well beaten out of us.

And at last only the man in the sweeping black cloak remained, and he was slowing in his attack, laughing breathlessly.

I half fell down two algae-greased steps, and plunged my head in to the water. Then, feeling strangely clear-headed, I bore down on the man in the black cape just as he collapsed to his knees from effort, breathing hard.

No doubt the great amount of wine I had swallowed encouraged me to fight. I half stumbled into Hubert's attacker. He looked up at me with a sweaty, carefree countenance, a quip on his lips. I pulled him the his feet. I clapped a hand on his shoulders and beamed into his face, like a long lost brother about to plant a kiss on his face.

He sought to run, and I would not let him go. He struggled, shrugged, squirmed, and I kept my grip, face to face with him.

It was a strange, delicious feeling to see fear light a man's eyes, and all because of the strength of my hands. I lifted the man from the ground by the fabric of is cape, a small man, under all his clothes, and a weak man, now that he was tired.

I could not suppress a troubling thought: how easy it would be to take his life.

chapter
SEVENTEEN

Birds sleep as we do, waking at night to cluck or purr, seeking reassurance. Then they puff their feathers, tuck back within their slumber, trusting that all is well. I watched the sleeping pigeons, wearing the cloak Hubert's attacker had left behind.

It was still night. I sat for a long time while Hubert vomited, held his head in his hands, and moaned. I kept watch along the street and the canal lest the reveling attackers rise up against us again.

Swallows stirred in the eaves, and I took comfort in the consultations the little fowl made, each to each.

"Great misery," said Hubert.

"If you can't stand," I said, "I can carry you."

"Carry me!" he said, as though the thought gave him shame.

Hubert felt along the wall as he walked, stopped to cough and to feel his ribs through his blouse. Each step he was like a man crossing fragile ice. I kept glancing back, expecting to see shadows slipping from arch to corridor, but a night watchman's voice lifted somewhere on another courtyard, and I wondered if some dark, blessed hour had arrived, when no man should stir beyond house or ship.

Hubert paused before a window, the wooden frame open like a door, and took a half step back, and bent low, peering.

"Glass!" he said at last. "Like my father's house in England."

The window frame was spanned with clear glass, and in the dim moonlight we could see our reflected forms, stooping and peering like dim-witted fools. The pane was lightly stippled, marred with a hint of bubbles, like beer.

No one stirred within, and the silence of the town was nearly perfect, except for our footsteps. When I spied a winesack full beside a sleeping man I lifted the wine and drank it all, every last swallow.

We scurried down an alley between casks and bales, and when a watchman challenged us, I responded, "Sant' Agnese," pronouncing the ship's name, and the name of our guardian saint, as I had heard the sailors pronounce the words.

The watchman held out a pike, in a cross-body stance, blocking our path. He wore leather armor with exaggerated, high shoulders, and a close-fitting iron helmet. The cross on his chest hung from a chain of gold and some lesser metal, gleaming with pretty menace in the starlight.

Beyond was a forest of ships and galleys tied to the wharf in the darkness. A heavy curtain swept my ankles behind me as I turned—the black, heavy cloak Hubert's attacker had left behind at his flight.

I felt within the cloak, and I slipped out a soft leather purse, lambskin, with a doe-hide drawstring. I pinched a coin in my finger, some foreign silver I did not recognize, but which I knew from its size and weight to be a quarter year's wage for even a Venetian pikeman.

"And a good night to you," I said.

With a swirl of the cape and a disjointed sensation of both triumph and stealth I strode up and down the wharf, and when another sentry challenged me I challenged him right back, with the name of our ship.

"In Jerusalem was my lover slain," I sang. *In Jerusalem watz my lemman slayn.*

A happy song, despite the mournful lyrics. I was sleepy, and the ship's deck slippery under my feet.

Strong hands gripped me from behind—stronger than those quick, light-footed Venetians. My own hands were held behind me, chains were brought, and yet again I was carried. I was beginning to enjoy the sensation, lifted along like a battering ram.

When I woke again I could not move, and did not want to.

Hubert was chained beside me, a pale face in the dark. "I hear animals," he said.

Footsteps echoed on the deck above.

"Animals of every sort!" Hubert said.

I would die soon, I knew from the throbbing of my brain. To turn my eyeballs caused darts of green lighting. I rolled to one side. If I called for help no one would hear me, except to stick a spear into me and end my suffering.

"Edmund," Hubert whispered. "Are you all right?"

I pretended I did not hear him, not out of unkindness, but because my tongue was a dry flake, a fragile thing that would break if I sought to use it.

"I can hear you breathing," said Hubert, hopefully.

Each bone is my skull was a fragment. "I breathe," I intoned.

Hubert was right: we were chained in the ark of Noah, a vessel laden with duck and sheep, horse and hen, each creature with a voice, and using it.

Sudden daylight stabbed the dark. I closed my eyes tight.

Venetian voices laughed, commented, cautioned, each sailor unnaturally lively. The fine, dry sound of grass rustled somewhere in
the hold, and the fragrance of hay. Hooves continued to knock
and shuffle overhead. The ship settled, taking on its new weight.
Loops of cordage rustled on the decking, and the ship gave a dig-
nified start, moving unmistakably through the water.

And then the ship jerked to a halt, distant voices jabbering,
calling. Voices lifted, the churn of the tiller and splash of the
sweeps echoing in our confinement.

Captain Sebastiano shouted, cajoled, swore by Saint John and the
Sacred Blood. He had a laugh that meant *damn you to hell,* and another that meant *my soul lightens at the sight of you.* Bare feet pattered,
a horse somewhere raised a scream of disbelief. A rooster celebrated
what must be day, out there in the world of the living. Other creatures made guttural, expressive noises. Bears, I thought—or pigs.

When Wenstan brought us each a dish of smoky, oily ham, he
spoke in a low voice. "I have never seen Sir Nigel so displeased,"
he stammered.

"Will we stay chained here forever?" asked Hubert, with no
self-pity but with an urgent, personal curiosity.

"Forever?" asked Wenstan. He considered—or perhaps he
paused because of his stammer. "Nothing lasts so long."

"What happened to my cape?" I heard myself croak

"That rag you were wearing?" said Wenstan airily. "It has been
returned to its rightful owner, along with the money." Wenstan
had trouble with the last word. "The money," he repeated. "The
coins you stole."

"I stole nothing," I said, in my most knightly voice, but inwardly I crumbled.

"The night watchman," said Wenstan. "He recognized the
purse."

chapter
EIGHTEEN

I found the water barrel and drank deeply, scoop after scoop, until Hubert stepped in to lead me away.

Nigel affected not to see, standing with his hands on his hips by the tiller, a man challenging the weather to attack. Rannulf did not spare us a glance, working with Miles on his weapon kit, polishing his short sword and oiling the seams of his chain mail. The sailors would not meet my eyes, and I felt like Jonah, a man who brought such bad luck to his shipmates that he was fed to a giant fish.

Venice had vanished. A black range of cloud jutted from the north. The ship wallowed. The sea puckered and dimpled, but no waves lifted and the wind was dead. The air was warm, and scented with the smell of decay, almost sweet, although the nearest land was a bare hint far to the west.

We carried a cargo of pigs and horses, and enough other beasts to populate a farm. The unfamiliar steeds rolled their eyes and screamed through their noses, hysterical and dangerous to anyone who mis-timed his approach. The pigs were more phlegmatic but equally vocal, questioning, protesting. Their odor was bitter and very strong.

We had a few new passengers, too, among them a canon priest from Padua named Father Urbino, who sat with a leather bucket beside him. He emptied the contents of his stomach with the regularity with which a clerk dips a quill in ink. A, big, blond man, he had three rings on his fingers, one a pink coral carved into a sacred image, the other two pink gold.

Christendom was attended by ordinary priests, who lived under one roof, and traveling priests, who were free to walk the land. Such traveling priests were often scholars and the sons of gentlemen, and so I appreciated the kind smile Father Urbino gave me. A few Frankish knights had joined us as passengers, too, along with their squires. The deck was a jumble of ration bags and lances.

The duty was punishment, but I was happy to be around the animals. Hubert and I bucketed salt water over the feces and urine of these bleating, squalling creatures. Our own horses, including Shadow and Winter Star, heard the newer animals snorting and joined the chorus.

The sailors swung mauls, large wooden hammers, pegging down hatches. Scoops and pails, rope and awl, any tool or tether that was not lashed or stowed was spirited away into the hold, which was already filled with sacks of wheat flour, oats, and cubits of hay.

Partly out of anxiety about what I saw in the sky, and partly to discover Nigel's humor, I said, "Hard weather is descending," in what I thought was a seaman-like turn of phrase.

Sir Nigel did not look my way, leaning against the side of the ship, paring his thumbnail with a small and shiny blade. "What a foul smell swine have," he said over his shoulder to Rannulf.

Rannulf made no comment, at work on his shield strap, kneading it with oil. Miles sat with him, soothing a whetstone across the blade of a knife with an ivory handle. I envied Miles at that moment, garbed in the same dark cloth Rannulf was wearing.

"I owe you and all aboard this ship my humblest apologies, and I beg, unworthy though I am, your mercy." This was my speech, and I had prepared it with care. I knelt on the deck.

"The cape and purse belonged to a nephew of the Doge," said Nigel. "The duke, the lord of Venice—you took his nephew's silver."

The lord duke has a bitch's whelp for a nephew, I wanted to say. "I mistook him for another sort of man entirely," I said.

Nigel stopped paring his thumbnail and gave me a look of keenest interest, as though an ox had uttered a proverb. "You judged a duke's son and found him wanting?"

I cautioned myself to be the perfect squire—in speech, if not in deed.

"They would have kept you in chains." said Nigel, "but Captain Sebastiano and I convinced them to forgive an errant Crusader."

Father Urbino wished me a good evening in heavily accented English. "She goes well," he said.

The ship, I assumed he meant. He spoke as a man greets his social inferior, politely but with simplicity. "Yes, Father," I agreed, "she goes very well."

Father Urbino glanced around, like a man accustomed to a servant. I took the slop bucket from his hand and emptied its contents over the side.

Actually, the ship was not going very well at all. The air was sultry, and the ship lolled and lurched slowly in the dull sea.

"We will arrive in time to kill many," said Father Urbino. He made a stabbing twisting gesture with an imaginary sword. "Many heathen."

I had often wondered what it was like to have a vision of Heaven. Did the beings in the presence of God have bodies like ours, or were they made of light and color? A nobleman could have asked a priest like Father Urbino, and the good Father would have spent hours explaining the celestial host.

I scrubbed and washed the deck, mopped and dried the planks, and then scattered dry straw. I was sweating like a man stunned with fever, like my poor father and mother, in their last illnesses. I did not like to draw a deep breath, the air sick-sweet, like burning sulfur.

The sea slackened completely, like canvas stretched across a floor, irregular as wrinkles passed through it.

Winter Star whinnied, and I called to silence him. The horses stirred and settled behind their wooden enclosure, and a pig set up a low-voiced conversation, swine speech that was nearly human, curious and apprehensive.

It struck just after sundown.

One moment we chewed duck bones and bread, and drank a sweet green wine, the ship still and quiet in the water. And then a single rope on the mast began to stir. It fell from its knot and swung, twitching.

It was only rope, I thought, and soon a sailor would lash it back into place. But the blind rope end searched, and probed, a restless serpent. Surely, I thought, someone will see it. Surely it means nothing, this single restless thing on a stagnant sea.

The rope was swinging, idle but unceasing. and the next instant the vessel yawed, plunging. She rolled to her side. The rigging shrieked.

94

The rope whipped through the dark. It caught a sailor in the skull, and the man went down spinning across the wet deck. I seized the wild rope and held it. I called for help. As a wave burst over the ship, my grip on the rope was all that saved me.

Two sailors joined me, clinging to the knot, and then Miles, skittering and falling, slid across the deck, into the foaming scuppers. And over, into the sea.

A dozen men cried out. The ship's stern swung wide, and the *Sant' Agnese* staggered, broadside to the force of the storm. Sheep and pigs fell hard against their enclosures, horses struggling.

Sailors struggled to their posts, figures hunched and featureless in the dark. I wrapped my arms around the mast and hung on. Someone climbed toward me along a man-rope across the deck. It was Nigel, and he put his lips to my ear and yelled, "Help with the oar!" *Holp with the loof.*

"Miles is gone!" I cried.

I could hear Nigel call something, his hot breath on my ear, but I could not make it out.

"Miles is in the water!" I cried.

Nigel's features streamed, rain and brine.

Men wrestled with a great oar, more massive than the normal tiller, struggling to work the implement through the tiller-lock, and into the sea. The Genoan, for all his size, could not manage it, and the other sailors, strained and pulled, no more capable than monkeys.

I took a grip on the large tiller-oar, and we all strained to steer the ship stern to the wind, as seething water tumbled, threatening to roll her over.

As I turned my head, with effort, I saw Miles, waving, vanishing and waving, closer than before, his mouth a gash.

————

Later I told myself this wasn't possible. The night was too dark, my eyes burning with salt. Surely this was another apparition, yet another shadow in our wake.

Besides, what spar or wine cask could I throw him? The deck was stripped of everything not tied down, and as I called for Miles, another figure tumbled into the sea, a sailor. I was certain a sailing man would be able to swim, and I called out encouragement, my voice a shriek.

A hand lifted from the stewing water like a farmer, bidding on a prize ewe.

At that last moment, I thought: I know that face, that shoulder, those fingers reaching upward.

And then he, too, was lost.

chapter
NINETEEN

We took turns at the storm-tiller, Nigel and Rannulf joining me, each of them stouter than most of the sailors. Following seas climbed over her, and the *Sant' Agnese* trembled and staggered under the weight.

Hubert took his turn at the tiller with the rest, but he was not stout enough to make much difference. At one point in the long night one of the animal pens shattered, cut down by a heavy wave. Boards and corner-shafts flew, and starbursts vanished into the wind—hens and ducks. Sheep scattered, legs out, rolling, bleating, failing to find any purchase on the slick, heaving deck.

I shivered, gripping hard when it was my turn at the tiller again, and at last, as dawn was breaking, the sky begin to lift. Tatters of dark cloud hung down, the storm dissolving, sunlight lancing.

But the seas remained heavy, and at last Rannulf and I were together, clinging to the tiller. I hung on with a stony stubbornness, but Rannulf leaned into the oar as though he took pleasure in the strain.

I wanted to offer condolences at the loss of his squire, but his bearded face was forbidding, his eyes on some far-off point.

———

Horses soon forget.

Hours of sunlight and calm winds, and Winter Star accepted my caresses and a feedbag of oats. For Winter Star, nothing troubling had ever happened. More than half our livestock had vanished, however, and the pigs discoursed, querying me as I walked among the horses, insisting on my attention. I gave their bristly, swelling bodies a pat, their skin pink and wrinkled under the wiry white-and-brown hairs. The pigs chewed bread crusts and fish heads, contented with what human stomachs had not been able to take in.

I found that Miles's clothing fit me, cut at the sleeve, and stitched, as one of the sailors was pleased to do. I knew that I wore a dead man's kit, and heard a dead man's song in my soul, the lay of a man dressing like a fox to creep closer to his lady's doves. Such songs are so often of unfaithfulness, encouraging the married baron to dally with some duchess across the dale.

I wore Miles's knife. The ivory-handled blade fit in a scabbard Hubert gave me, leather from the skin of a mare, a gift I felt unworthy of accepting.

Men do not forget so soon. Father Urbino spoke the noble Latin, praying to God for the rest of the souls of our brothers Miles de Neville and Matteo Mattei, the big sailor from Genoa. It was not a formal requiem, simply a brief address to Heaven. Only a few of the sailors were able to gather. Two were joint-wrenched, injured by falls during the storm. A few had a flux, black water in the bowels.

Father Urbino was a wraith, unshaven, shadows around his eyes, his *Spiritui Sancto* a thin, quavering tenor.

"With your pardon, Father," I said, holding out my hand. I dropped a gold ring into his palm, and as he stared at it in wonderment I closed his fingers around it.

Gold is sunny and warm. It does not tarnish in a night, and the goldsmith taps his hammer lightly, melts his bullion easily. Gold is agreeable, easy of love, and for all this I prefer silver.

"It fell, Father," I said. "From your finger."

"My fingers—they grew thin and wrinkled overnight," he said. "Many thanks!"

"The day—the wind the sun—will be good now," I said, in the childish formal talk we use with children and people who do not share our tongue.

"Good to us, bad to God's enemies," said Father Urbino.

Wenstan could barely make a sound. When I put my arm around him he merely turned away, and gazed down into the wake of our ship. The storm tiller had been replaced by a more slender device that cut the sea like a butcher's knife.

"I despised him for his songs," stammered Wenstan. "But now—" He took a deep breath. "Now I miss him like a brother."

"We'll kill a hundred Infidels in vengeance," I responded.

Wenstan offered me a pained smile.

"Tell me of the wonders of the Holy Land," I suggested, to take his mind off his sorrow.

He shook his head.

I beseeched him, and he shrugged. "They have the True Cross in Jerusalem," said Wenstan, in a soft voice.

I leaned close to hear him.

"The pagans have it," he continued, speaking carefully to still his stammer. "And they will not let it free to the Christians. That's one of the reasons we are called there."

"But surely there are bits of the True Cross in England," I said, happy to hear him talk of some sunny subject.

"Fragments—little pieces, like the Rood of Bromeholme. But the length and breadth are in Jerusalem, hostage."

A gull hunted in our wake.

chapter
TWENTY

The next morning I woke with a start.

I did not know where I was. The pallet straw crackled under me, the floor lifting gently, falling.

I had thought I was a boy again, my father out tending the goat, my mother bustling, feeding twigs to the fire. My early childhood had been filled with the bright perfume of stave sap.

On deck I hurried from side to side, drinking in the sunlight. The bright penny of light in the sky was not its ordinary gold— it was blue, like the finest beaten silver. I laughed—the sea was furnished with islands, far-off hills that rose up out of the gentle carpet of the water.

It was as though a hand had set them out, arranged them all for a story lesson, like the sacred plays Father Joseph arranged, the Three Kings traveling from the East to kneel before Our Lord. A distant boat drifted like a gnat in a currentless, glassy patch of sea. Even at the distance I could make out the gauzy brown hand of the net reaching, falling, vanishing into the deep.

The livestock enclosures had been re-pegged and lashed, and Winter Star whinnied at the sight of me, accepting the feedbag eagerly. There is something very pleasing about the sound of a horse chewing, the strong teeth pleasuring in the rich grain, a crunch like footsteps in snow.

I helped the deck hands wash down the wooden planks, mopping and scrubbing. I had rarely felt such inexplicable joy, the sun so warm I was sweating through my tunic. The ship was pungent with animal piss, and another, more severe scent, black flux, a fever that struck its victims with astonishing swiftness. The ship's surgeon, a man who looked smaller and less capable than any of the other seamen, emptied a slop bucket and hurried back to his patients.

"Today I am mastering the sword!" I told Hubert when he appeared, yawning and wan.

"You handle it well enough already," lied Hubert cheerfully.

"I fight like a milkmaid. Get your shield," I said. "Unless you are sick." Indeed, there was glaze of sweat on his face, and he blinked in the morning light.

"I'm sore, skin and bone," said Hubert, accepting a cup from one of the sailor-servants. He swallowed wine and water, and looked out at the sea. "Are you quite well?" Hubert asked.

Nigel and Wenstan were meeting with Captain Sebastiano near the mast. The captain folded his arms and did not speak. He shrugged, rolled his eyes. He lifted his palms in bewilderment.

Nigel's gestures became sharper. At last he turned away, his mouth twisted, spitting curses. Rannulf pointed to the south. He gestured toward the east, a show of reasonable discourse. Captain Sebastiano gazed up at Heaven, and gave a sigh of apology, unable to make out a word.

"I'll put his head on a pike," said Nigel. "And all his sailors, too."

Rannulf said something in a low voice.

The captain wore a thoughtful, inward expression. The storm had left him looking calm but suspicious. He gave an order, and bare feet padded quickly off into the stern.

A sailor arrived with a rolled parchment, tied with gold cord. Knots were untied, and the chart was spread on the deck, the corners anchored with lead weights. Nigel knelt, reached out a hand, but the captain stopped him from touching the wine-blue and beetroot-red shapes, a map of Christendom.

Rannulf knelt, too, both knights following the captain's finger with their eyes. "The east," said the captain. He indicated a spot in the empty sea. "The ship," he said.

"I don't understand this," said Nigel. He glanced at Rannulf. "Do you?"

"It's a chart," said Rannulf.

I drank in the glory of this map, an angel at each corner, golden wings spread wide. "This is England!" I said.

The two knights looked at me with surprise.

"And here," I continued. "This city on the hill—this is Jerusalem!"

"The wind," Nigel confided to me. "The wind blew us father than we thought."

"Are we off our course?" I asked.

Nigel smiled. "Let us say that there are bad accidents," he said. "And good ones. We are much closer than we thought."

Hubert forced his head into his helmet, and worked his arm through the shield straps. The helmet forced his features into a frown, and made him look like a stranger. The sailors who were healthy enough arranged themselves against the sides of the ship. I hefted my gray steel blade, took a slice out of the air.

Hubert teased the point of his bright sword toward me in the sunlight, and I took a mighty whack at his shield, letting the sword clash loudly against the blue Crusader's cross. And I laid on another stroke, in sport, but determined, too.

Hubert staggered, tossing off a little laugh of unconcern. I hit him again, and he nearly went down.

Sailors called encouragement, clapping. The Frankish knights and their squires smiled noncommittally: so now we shall see how these English fight. I scented the warm horseflesh, the fermenting hay, the tarry cordage, and the sour wine. I smelled the ocean, like sweat and iron. I caught the perfume of fish frying somewhere out of sight, and the humid, soiled bedding of the sick.

Hubert's eyes were a source of light, illuminated from within as he pressed the attack, his shield against mine, pushing. A sharp burst of pain in my bowels crippled me. I hunched over, unable to take a breath.

I twisted, sure someone had knifed me from behind, but there was no one there, and no wound. Nigel parted his lips to speak, and the sky quaked, like a great blue sheet held across us all, unevenly drifting to cover the ship.

I straightened, panting, my hands cold and wet, and managed a laugh of apology. The sword was heavy, the point scraping across the wooden deck.

Hubert hesitated, a question in his eyes.

"Come on!" I cried.

Gingerly, Hubert took a half-step forward. A pig made a guttural sound, and another pig responded. A horse shied within the enclosure, as I took an exuberant whack at Hubert's shield.

And slipped.

I stood at once, but my knees were weak, and hot fluid streamed down my legs. Blood, I thought. I am cut and bleeding!

But the smell was the rank odor of feces and fever, and I stood, wobbling, tracking brown, watery footsteps across the deck.

chapter
TWENTY-ONE

Sweet malmsey wine was pressed to my lips, and a cold cloth wiped my face.

I was burning, tearing at the blankets, unable to draw an easy breath. And the next moment I was icy, frozen through to my liver, my teeth chattering.

Father Joseph used to say that suffering, even squalid illness, was a gift from God. I knew that this fever was sent from Heaven, a reminder that I was the apprentice of a counterfeiter, little better than a thief myself. I was an ordinary young man with no good name, unworthy of the battle for the True Cross.

I slept, a stew of dreams. Other sick men were in this lower deck with me. I could hear them groaning. Their breathing grew slow and thin, and then the rattle began, the dry kernel of life in their throats. One man sat up, exclaimed to Santa Maria, and expired.

The ship's surgeon wrung out the cold cloth, and pressed it to my forehead. "All will be well," he said, in wooden English, words I knew he was repeating without comprehension. *Alla willa bee.* He was a thin, sweating man, breathless from his rush from one patient to another.

I dreamed I was home, beside the hearth, Elviva laughing as I told her the story of the vixen who spoke to the woodsman. In the warm, happy refuge of the dream I said I had heard it from a cheese-man. Her father chuckled to see Elviva smile, and Otto laughed, saying that no cheese-maker could be believed or trusted.

It was not like a dream. It was like one of those times that had really happened, one of the evenings I longed for, hearth and conversation, mending a bellows or drinking green ale. Rain in the thatch overhead, all well, all safe.

You chop against the oak's grain, the vixen had advised. There in the firelight I asserted that if a vixen spoke she would say something of much greater interest. She would speak of love.

Now I could see Elviva's green eyes, and I felt a great desire for her.

The monk's wife, they call it, the sort of love-dream that leaves the sleeper with a warm wetness at his crotch. I woke, and already the dream of Elviva was dim, was gone.

Rannulf crouched beside me, kneading leather-soap into his gear, polishing, working steadfastly, hour by hour. He worked neat's fat into my shoes, and restitched the hem of my clothes. When I caught his eye he offered a smile with his scarred lips.

"It won't be long," he said.

How many days and nights had I been so feverish? I parted my lips to ask, and he held a cup of wine to my lips. The fragrant liquor filled my nose, the astonishing sweetness flooded me, and I could not ask.

"I'm sorry," I rasped.

Rannulf's eye said: for what?

"For being such a useless squire."

"A squire with a strong arm," Rannulf replied, "who can read a ship's chart—at what exactly are you useless, Edmund?"

Was it morning, I wondered, or early evening?

Golden light flowed through the planks into my close, sweaty darkness. Soon, an inner voice mocked me.

Soon bone, soon dust.

The ship was silent, and it was unmoving.

Even the dying had been taken away. No footstep above on the deck, no laugh, no word.

What a wheedling, thin voice I had! I sounded older than Goodwife Anne, the venerated franklin's widow, who lived in a house of black timber and white clay. My master Otto would always lift his voice when he wished her good morning, and she would quail back, "Good morning to you!" in a voice that was nearly inaudible.

I crept like an old woman. Sunlight streamed into the dank corner, and I blinked as the illumination from the sky fell over me, blinding me. Hands seized me, voices were calling to me.

"Come out," Hubert was saying, "Edmund, come out and see!"

"Easy with him," said Nigel.

Hubert half dragged me, "Hurry, Edmund—come look!"

I tottered, Hubert's grip on my arm. The late afternoon sky was bright enough to make me cringe. The rank odor of my own body within its sweat-dark tunic rose around me. I was not alone after all—everyone was silent, leaning over the ship's side, gazing eastward.

I blinked, my vision hammered by the blue sky and sun-gilded sea.

A city of boats, ships, pinnaces, galleys, freight hulks, shore coracles, stretched in every direction. The ships were anchored, and the shore boats darted and skittered. The water was quick-calm, every stern reflecting a scribble of light.

Beyond was the shore. An ocean of tents met the sea, peaks and spires of every color, butter-yellow, steel-blue, the tiny figures of man and knight among the multicolored dwellings.

The murmur of the crowd reached us: the smith-hammers, and armor-menders, the coughing, cursing, order-obedient host, thousands of men. The host surrounded a great castle, with towers and walls of gray stone, nearly lapping up to the sides of the castle, except where a desert of clawed land surrounded the walls.

And beyond it all rose the hills and trees, the slopes and shadows of a kingdom, birds and pasture land, sun-naked trails and cloud-shadowed field. The farthest hills were as stone blue as the evening that rose slowly into the sky from the east. Cooking fires began to wink on, joining the forge coals sending white smoke in rising columns, over the great army.

chapter
TWENTY-TWO

The white sand glittered, gently wind-contoured and un-marred by any hoof. Pebbles glittered, not round, like river stones, but jagged, every shade of autumn gold. When the wind blew across the dunes it whispered, like bare feet running through summer rye.

A week had passed, and I felt strong again. Each breath I drew was sweet. Each sound, whether beast or man, was a cause of fascination, or promise. Even the spill of surf along the sand, white ale suds winking and fading, was a wonder in my eyes.

Hubert toyed with his reins, waiting for me to catch up.

Acre was a fortress city on the edge of the sea. The Holy City of Jerusalem was a day's ride east, but the enemy held all the inland territory. Nigel had explained to me that first we had to win Acre, and then we would have the honor of fighting our way toward the Holy Sepulcher in Jerusalem.

"We'll race," Hubert was saying, "to that little black spot on the beach."

I shielded my eyes against the noon sun. I could make out three Frankish knights exercising their mounts upon the long slope of the beach, and a galley mast that had washed up overnight, a black, gleaming spindle tangled in rigging. Don't ride far, Nigel had cautioned.

The great wooden siege engine was being repaired, and there would be a show of force early that evening. The siege engines were wooden towers that could be rolled across the ground, all the way to the enemy walls. Men could step from the top of a siege engine onto the enemy battlements. I had been practicing with my broadsword every day. Exercising the horses was not mere sport—Hubert and I had run all the warhorses up and down the beach, each charger wild-eyed and unpredictable after so long at sea.

But my anticipation of battle was a source of unease. True, I wanted the excitement, and yet I also wanted the adventure of battle to arrive and depart quickly. I wanted it to be over.

"That little speck, with the gulls beside it," Hubert was saying.

Hubert's horse Shadow danced, and then he was off. Gouts of sand kicked up by hooves drifted, sifting downward in the wind.

Winter Star skittered sideways. And then he ran, too, still overeager after days on land, kicking out at nothing, capering, snorting. He galloped hard for a while, stretching out his neck, the wind streaming in my hair.

And then Winter Star veered, pounding up the dunes toward the hills, flinging sand behind us, bucking, prancing—in entirely the wrong direction.

I reined him in and waited while Hubert galloped up, Shadow sweating and heaving. Winter Star and Shadow nosed the air toward each other, touching. Despite Winter Star's fiery unreliability, he was becoming strangely good-natured. He timed his bites to miss, usually. The only man he had kicked since we reached the siege of Acre had been Sir Guy de Renne.

The Frankish men-at-arms had been joined by others, a small band of knights and squires talking and joking, viewing the spectacle of Acre.

"The speck is still there," he said. "Maybe it's a cheese—the gulls are fighting over it." Cargo did sometimes drift to shore, thrown overboard by ships attempting to outrun raiding galleys.

The Frankish knights did not see it yet, a small round object at the very edge of the surf. I could already guess what it was, and nearly cautioned Hubert, but he was off, and Winter Star bolted after him.

Our race had caught the attention of the Franks and they watched, commenting, calling derisively.

Winter Star did as I wished, ran hard, and stopped when I wanted, with a toss of his mane. Was it possible that Winter Star was showing off, I wondered, aware of the Frankish horses?

Hubert wrinkled his nose, and at first I thought he might be making a comment about the unseemly catcalls of the Franks. Hubert's mount was breathing hard. A gull shied away reluctantly, studied us, then flew along the beach.

A blackened, eyeless human head grinned up at the sky.

"A Saracen," I said, "from one of the galleys in the battle last evening."

I swung down from Winter Star and knelt, holding my breath against the stink.

Four Pisan galleys had run in last night, through a screen of Saracen warships Saladin had set up in recent days, hoping to prevent the arrival of King Richard. One of the Moslem ships had caught fire, and burned past midnight.

I was dizzy, still a little weak from my illness. But I had been much fortified by roasted hen and guinea fowl since our arrival, not to mention chunks of the huge wheels of brown bread the

Templar bakers produced every morning. The bread was gritty and blemished with bug larvae baked in with the wheat, but it was delicious.

Flies were thick. I stretched out my hand, seized the golden ring around a dark nodule, the remains of an ear. I tugged. The head seemed to tug back, and I worried at the gristly lobe, twisting the gleaming yellow earring, until at last it popped free.

Hooves thudded, and we were surrounded by smiling Frankish knights, four of them, each with a squire. All of them beaming, showing their brown, wine-stained teeth. The broadest and tallest spoke to me in Frankish, and held out his hand, giving his fingers an inward twitch in the universal *give it to me*.

I stood, gave a respectful bow, and said, "No, my lord, if it please you."

Every Christian fighting man was hollow-eyed. This group was no different than anyone else in the Crusader camp, eager for the siege engines to do their work, and for the siege to break. Or maybe Saladin would bring his army in from the east, and engage in a battle—that was even more desirable. Instead, we exercised our horses, kept an edge on our weapons, and prayed that camp fever would not strike us down.

Every Englishman and many of the Franks prayed each evening for King Richard's safe arrival.

A distant roar made us all turn. Even at this distance we could hear the cheers of anticipation. God's Own Sling, the catapult owned by the English Crusaders, had been re-employed after a shortage of good-sized boulders, and it was once again cocked, ready to loose its missile.

When the distant stone left its catapult the black ash rose, and slowly fell toward the tower-spiked walls.

It struck, and bounded free, and we waited until the sharp *tock* of the stone-strike reached us, and the cheers of the men. Not to be outdone, Evil Neighbor, the Templars' magnificent catapult, fired a boulder at the same tower, and we held our breath at this fine, black point of grit, a boulder it had taken three men to load, rose high. Its arc was beautiful, higher than any the English common-fund catapult could reach. The stone struck the same tower.

Tiny black fleas along the tower brandished weapons. But a fragment of tower—a shard the size of a man—crumbled and fell, and after a long pause the Crusader cheers reached us.

I had expected the Holy Land to be a place of miracle, angels at wellheads, saints in caves. It was even better than that. This was a land of wild thyme and date palms, huge trees with wooden plumes for leaves. Bees touched the flowering weeds, and hills lifted and fell to the east, bare of forest. The streams were but a trickle through black stones where they touched the sea.

The Frankish knights rode with us back to camp, bumping us insolently, begging our pardon with exaggerated courtesy. All the way through the women's camp at the edge, the Frankish knights ignored the dark-haired pleasure women, a dozen voices wishing us a good afternoon, come and stay a while. At the same time washerwomen told us in four different languages how dirty we looked, such strong men, all we needed was a clean vest under our shirts.

The fighting camp was a city of canvas, man-high tent pegs and taut ropes. The smells of horse, roasting beef, and human habitation met us—feces from the latrine trench, sweat from the laborers wielding mallets and mauls, re-pegging one of the oak-and-cedar siege engines.

The Duke of Burgundy had designated Sir Guy de Renne

chief steward of the camp. Guy de Renne had an amazingly upright posture, all the more remarkable in a man who appeared so quickly in one place and then another. Now he hurried up to the Frankish knights, scolding, wondering where they had been. The explanation they gave made Sir Guy turn to us and say, in a Frankish tongue I was beginning to understand too well, that sport among boys was all very well at home, with our English mothers.

A Frankish knight spoke, and the duke listened attentively.

Sir Guy was one of those rare men who look clean-shaven, no matter the time of day, and whose sword pommel is always polished bright. Sir Guy made his eyes round as his mouth, an unspoken *Oh!* He held out his hand toward me with the slightest smile.

"The gold, my little pup," he said. *L'or, mon petit chien.*

I was as tall as the tallest of these Frankish knights, and Winter Star, flaring his nostrils impressively, was obedient to my slightest touch—with luck. My master Otto had spoken a smattering of Frankish, and I could at least approximate the accent. But I was aware that these were accomplished fighting men—and I was not.

Nevertheless, I closed my fist around the golden earring and tried to give these knights a look of disdain. Sir Guy gave me a smile of such coolness—such arrogance—that I melted inwardly.

Winter Star had kicked him two days before, "near to splitting his brains," as Nigel had put it. But Guy had not lost a moment of consciousness, stood, brushed himself free of straw and dust, and walked on as though nothing had happened. Hubert was sure Guy never slept or passed water.

I felt unsteady, perhaps still light-headed from my illness. I was not accustomed to addressing knights. I held up the golden earring, letting the afternoon sun play along its unalloyed perfection, except for a little kiss of black, a touch of Saracen gristle. I made up some Frankish of my own right there, saying that this was mine "By the right of my hand," *le droit de main,* although, in the same breath, I begged their pardon.

Several English had gathered, pikemen, sallow Dovermen, who could hardly make out a word of any Christian tongue. And then two Templars strode into the midst of this small crowd, stern, indifferent men, looking at none of us, dismissing us without a word. The Templars and the Hospitallers, as every Christian knew, were religious fighting orders, knights who had taken holy vows.

From a far part of the camp an expectant buzz of voices spread. Then, a hush, and tiny, tight creaking of leather and timber as Evil Neighbor stretched, and stretched still farther.

A whiplash snap, and a boulder whistled upward, a sound like a thousand cock swallows.

A silence. A horse's tail whisked flies.

The boulder glanced off the tower face, with a shower of mortar and stone-sparks. The stone missile bounced away, a faint, spinning shadow. The Christian army cheered, but without as much life as before.

"Before nightfall" said Hubert, "I'm going to kill my first Infidel."

chapter
TWENTY-THREE

In the hours before battle we had sport.

Men wrestled, the stouter wearing down the lean. Men ran footraces, the short and quick outstripping the robust. My favorite contest was called thrashing the cock—a carter would put on a blindfold and lay about him with an ox whip, laughing but intent, and once or twice my ear was singed by the crack of the lash. Hubert was even more nimble, the whip never even close.

The army loved these games, especially the squires and the yeomen foot soldiers, but as the hour of battle approached our laughter seemed too loud, our smiles too bright.

Rannulf was in his tent, rubbing oil into the chain mail on his lap. This was my customary duty now that I was his squire, and I flushed with shame. I hurried to tell him why we had been delayed, sporting with the fighting men. It told him about the golden ring, placing it in his hand.

Rannulf held the circlet to the afternoon sun falling through the tent flap. "They're forbidden to play dice," said Rannulf, "and the camp women are cattle, so they look for English squires to stab or bugger."

A catapult sang out again, beyond the tent city. A taut, leather hum and a loud whiplash, followed by the audible hiss of a boulder as it rose.

We were both quiet, waiting. A crack, and the muted cough of wall crumbling just a little further into gravel.

Rannulf held up the coat of mail, the shape of a man. It made a pleasing, steely whisper as he let it collapse in his lap. "So our Frankish friends decided not to test their steel or their manly parts. That's a blessing for Edmund, whose sword work will cost him his life."

"Morning and afternoon," I said, "I work at my lord's pleasure." This was formula, phrasing I had learned from Hubert. Hubert explained that the great warriors of ancient days spoke thus, Achilles and Hector at the walls of Troy.

Hubert had been practicing sword fighting with me, teaching me with a weapon with two false edges and a rounded tip. Hubert had told me about the estoc, the knife for piercing mail when the enemy is wounded and lying on the ground. He taught me footwork, and even tried getting me to use a bastard sword, a hand-and-a-half model he thought might suit me better than a single-handed hilt.

Rannulf often thought for a long moment before he spoke. "Take that monstrous thing wrapped in horsehide, Edmund. See if it might please you."

A louse struggled slowly along the back of my hand. I pinched the tiny creature, breaking it between my fingers. My armpits itched ceaselessly, and the back of my neck was sore from scratching.

What looked like a tree branch sheathed in horse-neck leather rested on Rannulf's brass-worked war trunk. I lifted the heavy object tentatively, eager, curious and yet unwilling to unwrap it.

"It belonged to a giant of Saxony," said Rannulf. "Go on, don't look so suspicious—do you think I'd give you a gourd on a stick?"

The Saxons were all giants, armed with huge weapons. The massive men had been struck hard by the arnaldia, a disease that made fingernails fall out and filled the lungs with blood. Most of the Saxons had been shipped north to Constantinople on Venetian freighters, not expecting to survive the voyage.

I let the sleeve of leather fall free.

"I was hoping to be a swordsman," I said, before I could stop myself.

I was shaken at the scope and menace of the weapon in my hand. A length of black iron was fitted with a massive hammerhead. The head had been polished, and gleamed.

At times Rannulf's eyes were full of feeling. Should I have kept my silence? "I won't be able to fight with this."

"Lift it," said Rannulf.

I gripped the shaft. "I'll learn to fight with a sword—just a little more practice," I protested.

"Go on," he said patiently. "Lift it high."

I held the hammer upward, the head brushing the canvas of the tent. I swung it, a slow circle. Making a show of how easy it was, gritting my teeth against the effort.

And it was not so heavy after all.

Priests said mass that afternoon. The Devil must have wept to see such faith, under the high-lofted clouds. Through it all I tried not to feel what I was experiencing, a simmering fear. The knights looked like strangers, even the ones I knew well, mail skirts down beyond their knees, surcoats of wool emblazoned with the cross.

Sir Guy de Renne was radiant after mass, gazing Heavenward, tugging on his fighting gloves, finger by finger.

"A show of force?" Nigel was asking. Chain mail made a gentle, chiming whisper as men moved around us.

"Eh?" said Sir Guy, making a show of understanding not a word.

Nigel said a few words of strained Frankish, and Sir Guy smiled in a fatherly manner. "We shall disturb their sleep," he said in words all too easy to translate. "We shall worry their women—"

"We'll see a few of our men lose their lives," said Nigel.

"Eh?" Sir Guy wrinkled his nose.

The knights held back, letting the footmen carry the effort at first. A siege engine's axles were greased with ox fat, and the workmen stood aside cheerfully as Sir Nigel inspected the workings of one of the wooden structures. "You could put old women in this and it would serve as well," said Nigel.

The tower had served well in several assaults before we arrived, but each time the defenders killed the siege engine's passengers faster than the attackers could disembark through the summit. The last time the tower had been used, three days previously, it had caught fire because of hot coals hurled from iron braziers. The braziers were smoking even now, on the edge of the walls.

The foot soldiers, few of whom spoke English, stood expectantly.

"Go on," said Nigel, with a show of enthusiasm. "To the walls!"

The footmen gave their shoulders to the wheel and axle, and heaved. The great wooden tower creaked, rocking, crossbowmen standing by to mount the portable edifice.

It creaked again, timbers reporting up and down the tall shaft. But the wheels did not turn.

"Again!" cried Nigel. "To the walls!"

The siege engine rocked forward, and then caught speed, swaying, rolling ahead over the uneven ground, to a throaty yell from the army.

I reassured myself—this was a battle, and I was still very much alive. More than alive—every color was bright. Hubert was alive, too, breathing hard although he was standing still. The enemy fortifications were dark with men, and a few sling stones pattered on the ground, testing the range, smacking the leather armor protecting the men driving the engine forward. There was a teasing, dreamlike quality about both the Christians and the defenders.

A splinter of stone bounded all the way to where we stood, and Hubert picked it off the ground. He threw it back toward the city, then dropped his hands, as though he had done a forbidden thing.

Still alive—the thought in my sinews.

I knew that Nigel would prefer to wait for the long-expected arrival of King Richard. But the French King Philip and his countrymen, the Teutonic knights, the Templars, and the Hospitallers—the entire polyglot force—were tired of watching their hair fall out in clumps, a symptom of the fever that festered throughout the camp.

Several men scrambled up the interior ladder, the siege engine trembling like a living thing. Within moments the top of the tower was manned with arbalestiers, crossbowmen armed with short swords. Dozens of common soldiers, freedman haywards and foresters in their ordinary lives, gave a shoulder again to the wooden wheels, and the great tower advanced more quickly over the battle-leveled ground.

The strong men pushed the siege engine to the edge of the

cleared space around the walled city, protected from the eyes of the defenders by wood-and-leather shields.

Soldiers holding back, in the main force, carried a new device, something the Mussulmen had not seen before, a grappling ladder called "the cat." There were several similar, long ladders with specially smithed hooks at either end.

Another sling stone buzzed though the army, and struck a water-carrier on the ankle. The boy hopped on one foot, pretending to be injured, but also not pretending—really hurt. A weapon I had never seen before, a machine like a large crossbow, snapped projectiles high over the city walls, the leaden shot whistling.

The siege engine wobbled forward, the men in the top looking back and waving, like city fathers enjoying the view from a belfry.

Acre's defenders jeered, and sang challenges across the battered plain. The flattened earth around the city was broader than it appeared at a distance. As the siege engine groaned across the bare dirt, the attackers and defenders cried threats so menacing they sounded cheerful, as though a harmless tournament was being resumed at long last, to the relief of all.

The tower was moving faster now, the wheels squeaking, chattering.

Smoking coals spun through the air, and the men in the tower top smothered the embers with sand, stomping methodically. The siege tower was so close to the city now that the shadow of the tower fell over the defenders.

Arrows showered into the tower, and then, with a timber-splintering *whack,* the siege engine struck the wall.

It began to rain stones, glowing coals, arrows, and quarrels— the projectiles fired by crossbows. The siege tower shivered up and down its length, additional men charging across the bare ground, shouldering each other in a stampede to ascend the vault.

Hubert and I struggled ahead, too far in the rear of the advancing line to be close to the fighting. The ladder gangs attached the hook ends of their equipment to the walls, and then crumpled under the rain of rock and arrows, as though weary and curling up for a nap.

A dull avalanche of noise shook the air: stone against iron, spear against helmet, swords ringing, every blow striking metal or hard leather.

In the height of the din, a Frankish knight surmounted the walls from the top of the siege tower, as easily as a man stepping from a boat to a wharf. He stood there in full view of all, handsomely armored, his flat-topped helmet ringing as stones and arrows bounded off the iron.

There was something womanly, or priestly, about the way the mail shirt hung nearly to his ankles. He raised his sword as though to salute his enemy. He stood on the battlements, took a step, and then wavered, like a man lost in weariness, as spears and bricks bounded from his helm.

He spilled into the stone city.

chapter
TWENTY-FOUR

The sound deafened me—so many voices I could not make out a word.

We were all thirsty. Men around us passed leather sacks, drinking with care, lest a drop fall wasted to the ground, then drinking with abandon, guzzling. Hubert was yelling, and so was I, calling for the help of the Holy Sepulcher, for the blessing of Our Lady. As though Our Lord's hands were being spiked within the walls at that very moment, his ribs lanced.

Knights in battle wear helmets shaped like buckets, some with rounded peaks, some flat, but Hubert and I were dressed like foot soldiers, iron and leather bowls over our heads, chain mail up to our chins, our faces exposed. Hubert was blushing and sweaty with the heat, the pressure of the short helmet forcing his face into a scowl.

The roar continued, an unending cry from the attacking army, a ceaseless howl from the defenders. But it was hoarse, now shrill and not as loud. Crossbow quarrels hummed through the air from the Crusader ranks, shattering on stone, sometimes drilling into flesh. The first time I saw a wrist screwed through by one of these missiles I winced, and closed my eyes.

But soon I saw worse things. Men clambered up the ladders, paused to adjust their helmets, half drunk with wine. Stones and arrows sang off Crusader chain mail. One by one the Christian fighters slumped, laborers overcome with exhaustion, and either fell or were lowered back down, bleeding onto the shoulders of their companions.

When one of the new cat-ladders was pried at last from its grip on the walls, the defenders struggled to shove the contraption further away from the battlements. The ladder was thick with fighting men, shaking their weapons and cursing the defenders, who could not pole the ladder free from the wall. It all looked laughable in a sickening way, a market-day brawl among neighbors.

At last an infidel with bright yellow sleeves and a white head cloth leaned down over the battlement with a long spear and pricked the face, the cheeks, the eyes, of some of the pikemen, causing them to tumble like scarecrows down to the ground.

It all happened sluggishly, a battle among bees. Now and then helping arms carried someone through the armored men, faces streaming scarlet. Hubert and I lifted our cockcrows in the grand cacophony. Neither of us was close to the fighting, but we were lightly powdered with blood.

Rannulf stood nearby, watching with the calm concentration of a falconer observing his bird. Nigel had joined him, and the two shook their heads, shading their eyes with their hands.

Many of the arrows and leaden missiles that snapped through the air were Crusader in origin, saved up and now used against us. A heavy projectile shaped like a mushroom scarred the ground near Nigel, and he gave it a kick. When a Catalan squire ducked an arrow, Nigel laughed.

The sound of the hoarse cries altered, fell to a deeper timbre. Men turned around, and pushed and cajoled the siege towers slowly back over the now cluttered ground. The defenders showed themselves, shaking spears and fluttering their bright colors in the bronze light of the setting sun.

"A great battle," snorted Nigel.

I squirted red Tyre wine into Sir Rannulf's cup.

We sat on a thick carpet Rannulf had bought from a Burgundian, who had purchased it from a Cypriot, who had recovered it from a shipwreck. A clay oil lamp gave off a cheerful, delicately smoky light, and the carpet, a marvel of colors, was lightly glazed with salt and sand.

"I saved a squab for you, Sir Rannulf!" Wenstan stammered.

"It cost a Flemish obole," said Nigel. "Hard-bargained, but Wenstan would not pay more than that."

Three days had passed since the battle. Day and night it was too hot to think of further fighting. Hubert and I attended Nigel, which meant that we did little more than drowse in his tent, brushing flies from our eyes. We ate Templar bread and drank inferior wine, fit for squires, a beverage that had almost turned to vinegar. A rash on my skin seethed under my tunic, and I scratched until I bled.

Rannulf stabbed the gold-roasted bird with a knife, and held it into the candlelight. The bird was still spiked with pin feathers, its tiny, fire-withered head dangling. "The hens are gone?"

"Eaten, every one. A squab is fit food for a knight," said Nigel. "Chew up the little bird, Rannulf, and don't complain."

Rannulf pulled off a wing. "The pigs are eaten, too?"

"A Sicilian knight bought them all from our captain," said

Nigel. "He had a plan to render what was left after feasting, paste it on our arrowheads, and cause dismay among the Mussulmen."

"It would cause them misery," said Rannulf thoughtfully.

"But the pigs died of a murrain," said Nigel.

Rannulf had a way of absorbing news as though he had expected it all along. "The Frankish knights have questioned the prisoners," Rannulf said at last, stripping flesh off a slender, pink bone.

"And cut out their tongues afterwards," said Nigel, "no doubt."

Rannulf let the fleshless bone fall.

"Thin little devils, these Acre-men," added Nigel. "It's a wonder they fight as well as they do."

Rannulf concurred, using the Frankish *maigre*. "And thirsty. For water, never for wine."

Rannulf and Nigel discussed the mines sometimes excavated during sieges like this, tunnels that could be carved out under the foundations of the wall, and purposely collapsed. "But it will take too long," concluded Nigel. "The castle walls were built on rock fifty years ago—by Christians. Soon we will be roasting lice on a skewer for supper."

"Your squire is drunk," said Rannulf.

"Impossible," said Nigel, giving Hubert a nudge with his foot.

"I live to serve my lord," said Hubert thickly.

"I roasted a wood-mole once," said Nigel. "In the Forest of Galtre. My mount went lame. It was night, and raining, and the blind little creature wriggled out of his hole. I killed it with my glove, *whap*."

"One blow?" Rannulf asked.

Both men fell silent at the sound of a distant cry.

Nigel shook his head. "The women," he said. "Fighting again."

"We should drive all the camp followers away with whips," said Rannulf.

"They give us comfort," said Nigel. "Those of us who enjoy pleasure, Rannulf."

Several times at night a cry woke me, a wounded man with a fever, or a water boy having a nightmare. The camp stirred, hundreds of men awakened by the sound.

chapter
TWENTY-FIVE

Soon, we prayed.

Soon the King of England would set foot on this shore.

Rumor was alive. Richard Lionheart had left Crete, with a force of blue and yellow Genoan galleys. He was one day away, two at the most, with twenty galleys heavy with livestock and grain. He would arrive and attack at once. He would end the siege by midnight.

At the same time a devilish counsel nagged me: a wheedling suggestion that the king might not arrive at all, and that having seen one battle I could leave for home.

The catapults hammered the walls in the early morning, and then again in the late afternoon. One evening a crack appeared in a wall, like a rip in a blanket. Crusader bowmen and pikemen rushed forward with ladders, only to find Saracen masons already at work, hurling some of their building stones down upon our soldiers, more sleepwalker fighting, puppet men fighting men of straw.

Hubert continued to develop an amazing skill—he could imitate people. In the shade between the tents he would chirp,

"Who am I?" and do a killing mockery of Guy de Renne's upright posture, or Nigel's stiff-legged stride.

He had a further talent. In firelight he would make an animal out of his hands, throwing a shadow against the canvas. Whether hound or a serpent, each animal Hubert made had the same quality of quiet devilment. "What are you doing?" Nigel asked once, then crouched to watch. "A chimera!" he gasped. "Put your hands together like that again! A prime chimera, or I'm a sow."

"A chimera has three bodies, my lord" said Hubert, making the silhouette sprout ears. "This is only a roebuck. With a long tongue."

I made a silhouette of my own, a doe. The two shadow creatures goggled at each other, and Hubert and I fell to laughing.

Rannulf and I rode far down the shore, shadowed by the tiny figures of Saracen horsemen exercising their mounts and keeping an eye on us. They made me anxious.

"If they cut us from camp," said Rannulf, "then you'll see some fighting."

Rannulf carried a hunt spear—he had heard that a few lean lions prowled the briars of the Holy Land. "Even a warhorse would shy at the scent of a big cat," said Rannulf. "It would be hard to run down so much as a cub."

I had always been fascinated by lion lore. My master Otto had told me that the female lion bears lifeless kittens, and the male lion stands over the litter and roars it into life.

"Surely, my lord, a bow would have better luck."

"An iron-tipped arrow, it's true, but where's the courage in killing with an arrow?"

Rannulf flicked a small yellow flower from the sand with the point of his weapon, and kept it in the air, tossing it with his lance point. He speared a pink flower, and stabbed a spreading mallow weed. When at last he came upon a rodent burrow, a small hole in the dry earth, he stabbed his shaft into it, tearing up the ground. The torn earth had a pleasing odor, both fresh and fermented.

A tiny, tawny creature fled at last, escaping its wrecked home. Rannulf lanced at it, tiny as it was, and toyed with it, but the creature escaped whole and apparently unhurt.

I offered, "It's all in the balance, my lord."

Rannulf gave me a long glance, and I looked away, studying the long, straight line of the sea.

Fox spoor peppered a stream bank, delicate footprints and dung no bigger than a ferret's. A sheep's skull grinned from the flowering weeds, and the dry flock droppings told a tale of shepherds and a village, all the inhabitants fled.

I had long been tempted to ask, but only now could blurt the question, "Did you really kill so many as five men, my lord, at the famous tournament in Josselin?"

"My old friend Thomas fitzMaurice died of a fractured hip and back—his horse rolled when my charger collided with his. A rank accident. Three of my opponents, all good men, died over months of spoiled wounds, puffed up, turned black, and—" He shrugged heavily, his light leather hunting armor creaking. "I killed one on the field, a youth, younger than you—my horse trod on his chest. I killed five, and yet—" He shrugged.

Was I disappointed to learn that these deaths were not feats of sword?

"Men misjudge me," he said peacefully. "Inside, I sing songs like the ones Miles used to love, and I offer Heaven my own sort of prayers. Nigel is the one who craves."

"Craves, my lord?"

"He has an appetite. For women, and for battle."

Each morning Hubert and I trudged down to the water's edge, driftwood and shell underfoot, and gazed at the horizon for King Richard's ships. Often a Saracen galley crawled the distance, guarding the coast. Hubert and I had already adopted the knightly dislike for walking any distance at all. Very soon, Hubert opined, we should be allowed to wear spurs, like the knights from Aragon, who sat drinking claret wine in gold-and-indigo blouses, the rowels of their spurs gleaming.

Sometimes Hubert and I rode south of the camp, all the way to the dunes, and from there, if the wind had carved a hillock tall enough, we could see Saladin's armies to the east, tent peaks and fluttering standards.

Saladin's outriders coursed through the brush every day. They called after our Frankish horsemen, who galloped away, reined in, and galloped back in turn. The Saracens never fled quickly, always took their time, and the Franks were careful to stay well out of bow range.

Hubert and I pulled up short, Shadow and Winter Star breathing heavily. Today we had ridden farther south than usual, and the river stones scattered, dry and drought-scabbed. Water gleamed in the shade of a tree, spilling through green stones, and a Saracen knelt there, while his mount drank.

A horse can drink a long time, its belly filling, swallow by swallow. I often find it comforting, this heavy, meditative sound, water rising into the warm barrel of a horse's frame. The infidel stroked the horse's neck, smiling lightly, and only when Winter Star made a loud equine sneeze did the horseman glance and stand up, with no show of fear, or even curiosity.

I cleared my throat. "A pleasant afternoon," I offered.

Hubert looked at me out of the corner of his eye.

"And this," I continued, "is a peaceful place to let a horse take its ease."

The Saracen wore a deep yellow head covering, with a trailing cloth that hung down his nape. He was darkly bearded, and his teeth were white when he spoke.

Hubert sat tight in his saddle, like a chapel statue.

I made a gesture of apology: *I do not understand.*

"Francoman," said the Saracen. He indicated the two of us.

"Oh no!" I exclaimed. "Not Frankish. English. Two English."

He showed nearly all his fine teeth. English, French, his gesture said, what difference?

He pulled his charger gently from the stream, and indicated the water. Did I care to water my horse?

Hubert did not make a single move, although Shadow lifted his head, sniffing the unfamiliar horse.

I hesitated. If my throat was cut, I wondered, how badly would it hurt?

I dismounted, my feet whispering in the sand among the stones. The flesh of my throat, the pulse that trembled there— that was all I could think about as I led Winter Star to the stream. I let him nose the surface, shake his mane, bridle tinkling.

The Saracen was not as young as he had looked, a few gray whiskers in his beard, a scar like a red earthworm on his sword hand. Winter Star made short work of taking water, snuffled, pawed the sand, and looked intently at the Saracen's own mount.

The Saracen spoke, and I knew, without understanding the words, what he was saying.

I thanked him, and said that his horse, too, was fine. I added, speaking clear English, that the horse was not, in law, actually my own. It belonged to Sir Nigel, I said, although I myself was squire to—

Hoofbeats approached. The Saracen mounted his horse in an instant, and called out to his distant companions.

I stayed as I was.

Several outriders, from the sound of it, splashed and cantered through the water upstream.

Hubert wheeled, dug his heels into Shadow, so hard that the horse bolted. Hubert fought hard to master him long enough to turn back and call something strained and breathless.

The Saracen made a gesture to his forehead, and spoke. His voice was level, less friendly, now, but reassuring. He wished me well, let his horse mince like a lady's palfrey across the stream, and then rode hard to catch up with his companions.

"He could have quartered you, arms and legs, and put your head on a willow stick," said Hubert.

"But he didn't," I replied.

"There was your chance to run a pagan through to the heart," said Hubert, "and you traded by-your-leaves, like two wives at a fair."

"He was a knight-at-arms, at his ease," I said, using the lines from a lay about a knight outside his lady's garden, one of Miles's favorites.

Hubert urged his mount forward, and I did not follow him.

chapter
TWENTY-SIX

A well is a busy place.

No knight or squire, knight's clerk or priest would want to be seen drawing water. Serving boys carried the buckets, and washerwomen gathered, joking and singing in their foreign tongues.

Hubert ignored me, watching wrestling matches among the pikemen, practicing swordplay with a few Provençal squires. I found myself visiting the well all that afternoon, and much of the next day, and lingering, enjoying the gentle voices of the women.

When a friendship is interrupted, it is a shock, painful, as when the plow strikes a restharrow root, shaking the plowman to the bone. I consoled myself that I would do as well without Hubert and his piping voice, his eagerness.

But the thoughts were bitter, and they were lies.

I had never felt such heavy heat before, not on the longest summer day. Birds did not sing, and the sky paled, dust lifting to the very apex of the blue dome above. The rumor was that the wells in Acre were down to their last, black bottom moss.

I poured cool well water into a basin, a dented, tinker-wrought vessel. I washed my feet with a rag, and let the water trickle down over my face.

"Washing your skin?" said Nigel, his shadow falling over me.

I admitted that this was water, and that I was washing.

"No good," said Nigel, "can come of that."

"It is a hot day, if it please my lord."

"I knew a summoner who washed his hands and feet," said Nigel. "He caught a chill, and it went to his lungs, and he died."

"My lord, it cools the blood."

"This is what Hubert tells me—that your blood is as cool as a widow's."

I set my mouth, determined not to say another word. "If my blood is cool, then why do I feel the sun so?" I heard myself say.

"You have the mind of a shriver, Edmund."

I continued to rinse the rag in the cool water, and bathe my arms, although I took no pleasure in it, under Nigel's incurious, disapproving gaze.

"Smiths use water," I said, amazed to hear myself chatter. "To cool the tongs, Sir Nigel, and the red-hot iron."

Nigel sat and stuck a finger into the water. "Go to Hubert."

I scrubbed my face hard. "As my lord wishes," I said.

A few days ago Nigel would have laughed, one of his sharp, unthinking chuckles. He sighed, and after a long moment, he said, "Rannulf told Hubert he has all the sense of a pig's farrow. Rannulf told him that you and the Saracen knight were well met, and that in every way you acted like a man-at-arms."

I felt myself blush.

Nigel was quiet for a moment, listening to something far off. When I began to speak he put out his hand—*hush.*

Another brass instrument sounded, a strangled bleat at first— our horners were out of practice.

Then, a pure, golden tone.

More trumpets joined in, up and down the tent city. A washerwoman hurried from the well. A serving boy trotted off, careful not to spill his water at first, then failing, water splashing the dust.

I was on my feet, the basin overturned, water spreading at my feet.

We ran, through the tent city, to the beach, down the sand. I joined Hubert there, and we waved and cheered. Hubert and I helped Wenstan to loose a banner, a scarlet lion. And all the other squires shook free their flags, the lions, the dragons of silk, all of us shouting to be heard over the trumpets.

A force of blue and yellow Genoan galleys rode the tide, fending off a Saracen warship. "Twenty of them!" cried Hubert. "Thirty—and look how heavy they are in the water!"

A force of Saracen galleys, black oars beating in expert rhythm, swept down from the north.

Men began to kneel in the sand.

The city behind cried out with hope and horror, as the Saracen galleys scattered into the Genoan fleet. Ships collided, a low, gut-wrenching crash, great casks clashing, splintering. One Christian galley was holed at the waterline by the battering ram of the Saracen ship. Tiny insect-men swarmed, hacking and stabbing, as the remaining Genoan vessels broke free, white foam at their prows.

All that long day Genoan ships battled through the Saracen attackers, and one by one the Christian ships rode anchor, just beyond the surf. One of the Genoan vessels caught fire, and the reflection of the flames was beautiful, a carpet of gold on the dark water as the sun began to set.

The camp was noon-bright with bonfires, drift timber, masts, and staves piled on the beach and set alight.

"What does the king look like?" I asked.

"He's a tall man," said Hubert, "with a strong face. I'll know him as soon as I set eyes upon him."

Neither of us mentioned our disagreement, and it was forgotten between us. Knights waded ashore from the ships, the waves gentle, and each fell to his knees as soon as he reached the beach. The Templars, with their black-and-white blouses, were the only knights easy to identify in this firelight, all the rest of us sun-bronzed and indistinguishable from servants.

"That's him!" cried Hubert, as a red-maned, heavyset man staggered ashore, knelt to pray. The shaggy-haired man stood and called for wine, tugging at his clothes. He relieved himself copiously onto the sand, a man with the bladder of a stallion.

"He's the Duke of Ogilby," said a knight's clerk.

This duke was followed by a string of knights and barons, some of them drunk, some only half drunk, calling for a skinful of wine, each kneeling to pray before they staggered up on the sand to seize a proffered cup of the finest in the camp. Each man praised God for his deliverance, speaking Frankish. Each praised the saints and the Holy Cross as his squires and servants helped him up the beach though the bonfires to the camp.

But Hubert's face grew tense, and I had the same unvoiced fear—that King Richard was not with this fleet, that he was not yet arrived. Or worse—that he would never arrive, and that these fires of celebration would merely illuminate our disappointment.

"That's him!" Hubert would whisper, but each time it was William of Foy, or Alfred de Point, or Godwin of Shuckburgh. Or yet another William—of Dugdale, or Aston, or Essex. There arrived a full complement of earls and their squires, some of them not drunk so much as ill, weak-legged, some weeping with thanksgiving.

Torches were set alight, sputtering with rancid fat, and the black water was chased with gold and silver from the fires. Every man who could stand lined the beach, praising God, as at last a large galley, a dark shape, groaned against the sandy bottom, its keel cutting deep. An anchor splashed under the starlight.

Men disembarked, shadowy shapes. The wedge of knights and lords strode heavily through the water, and despite the throng an odd silence fell over us, thousands of men taking a deep breath.

The knot of men in gray and brown Norman wool stepped onto the shore, wet up to their waists. They fell to their knees.

All eyes were on one individual, a broad-shouldered, yellow-haired man, with a thick, muscular neck, and a face set in pious thanksgiving, or weariness, or some inner brooding. He prayed a long while, as an army of men watched, firelight flickering.

He rose to his feet, looking around at us, like a man surprised to see his servants still awake so late. He smiled, his eyes sweeping all of us, looking into the face of each fighting man and squire at a glance.

The king of England drew his sword. In the brilliant light, and in the thunder of our cheers, we could not hear his words.

chapter
TWENTY-SEVEN

To Jerusalem.

Before our cheers faded King Richard sheathed his sword with difficulty, his bodyguards closing ranks around him. The king made way toward the camp, bonfire sparks snapping. And as he left the sand and reached the solid ground, he staggered.

King Richard leaned into one of his guards and did not take another step. The army fell silent. Something about our camp displeased the king, we thought. And what was worse, as Philip, the king of France, made his appearance, Richard slumped, his knees buckling.

The king of France waited, while the king of England's men propped him up.

King Philip was a royal presence we rarely actually saw, a man who had fretted his days, waiting for the arrival of his English counterpart. The French king began to speak, some royal formula of greeting, but King Richard bent over with a groan, his knees giving out from under him.

At dawn the day was already hot.

The foot soldiers put their shoulders to their catapults, the mangonels, and the crossbowmen counted out their quarrels.

All the soldiers, Florentine and Brementine, Bourdeaux and Breton, worked with new faith, in the growing sunlight. The magnificent devices creaked and swayed to a predetermined line at the edge of the bare ground.

The machines began to hurl their projectiles not at the towers full of watchful sentries, not at the gate bruised and divotted from a hundred strikes, and not at random places in the walls. The catapults pounded a single point—the large, patched crack.

Blow after blow crumbled the new masonry, each strike crushing stone to grit. The chief builders of the city hurried across the battlements, ducking whenever a projectile soared. They took their positions again after the boulders punched yet another weak place in the groin of the crack.

The laboring men of Acre hurried, their heads in white cloths visible over the battlements. The catapults sighed, grunted, held their strength, tense and hard. And snapped, the boulders streaking toward their target. Wall stone rose into the sunlight, transformed into so much flour, crumbling to nothing. All day new yellow mortar clay was trowled into the huge crack that snaked, ever lower, down the face of the wall.

A whippet, newly arrived, hunted nervously from tent to tent. I reached out, and the trembling dog's nose touched my fingers. Evil Neighbor groaned like a ship in high seas, and then it was silent—the taut, prime silence that sent a thrill of anticipation.

With a heart-stopping crack the boulder spun upward, stopped spinning, high in the sky. And began a counterspin, a graceful pirouette, as it fell with a crunch against the wall.

———

Wenstan began to sing again, as he went upon his chores, beating the carpets, instructing the servants, inspecting the washerwomen's efforts. At first he merely hummed, the lay of the turtle dove, pining for the love of a cock-hawk. Then he sang entire verses, the song of the Battle of Jericho.

For over a week King Richard did not leave his tent. His bodyguard wore long skirts of fine wool past their knees, over dark, fine-mesh mail. The men sweated in the heat, unmoving when flies searched their faces, although not one of them could stand still when these fierce, hungry inspects approached their eyes.

Surgeons left the tent with samples of the king's watery stools, and the army was alive with rumors—that the king was black with boils, that the king was paralyzed by an ague, that an angel with a sword of snakes and green fire had strode through the camp, calling King Richard's name.

Each day Evil Neighbor and God's Own Sling powdered the walls, and all night the brickmen and the expert builders repaired the damage. A warhorse belonging to a Corsican nobleman collapsed in the hot sun, and had to be butchered, his flesh roasted, rib and haunch, over a fire.

The outriders killed a Sicilian lord who made the mistake of giving a three-year-old horse its head, rode too far, and made it back to camp pincushioned with barbed arrows. One morning before dawn a raid of Saracens nearly drove off our mounts. Two sentries were wounded. Priests hurried into their tents where surgeons tried to muffle their groans. The two guards died before sundown the next day, and Hubert said that the Saracen spears were poisoned, and their arrows barbed so they could not be extracted.

The camp bent to its work, no one resting in the shade, the

140

whetstone wheels singing, the armorers' fires glowing. Acre was intent, too, its sentries no longer calling challenges.

Saladin's army took a new position, closer to ours. The red and blue tents were rich hued in the afternoon sun, and the out-riders rode closer, riding along our line, counting us. Sometimes two or three of them stopped well within bowshot and gazed at the distant sea, as though our tents, our horses, our entire army had already vanished.

chapter
TWENTY-EIGHT

Heathen men began to escape from Acre.

Their shapes half fell down a rope, or climbed as careful as spiders. The deserters huddled in the moonlight, and then sprinted, full-out, all the way to our camp.

Our sentries threw them to the ground, trussed them. Word seeped through camp that the citizens of Acre were boiling sandals and chewing the cart frames for nourishing glue.

"Look what I found!" Hubert whispered one hot noon. Evil Neighbor was taking a rest, and the dust of the camp was settling, a fine, white second skin over every surface.

I was washing my hands and my feet, a habit I could not break. Hubert carried a copper bowl, and set it upright in the dust.

"What do you think I have here?" he asked.

"A piece of poor work," I said. "I could smith a better copper bowl with my eyes shut."

"What's inside?" he said, moving the bowl just out of reach.

"A Saracen's ear," I suggested.

Hubert spilled the contents of the bowl onto the ground, and a black, jet-shiny creature, all hook and claws, skittered forward.

I gazed at it with curiosity. Hubert laughed.

"Wenstan says the scorpion is a good omen," said Hubert.

"Omen of what, exactly?"

"The scorpion stings itself to death—everybody knows that," said Hubert.

"I'll bet you a penny," I responded, "that your fine scorpion will not sting itself."

"Soon it will die of its own poison," said Hubert.

The creature twitched, stinging upward, stabbing the air. Scorpions and spiders, vipers and centipedes were created when God cast Adam and Eve from the Garden. The sun multiplied such beasts from rot, decaying wood, and flesh. In God's innocent, unfallen Creation, no such creatures existed.

"What does it mean," I asked at last, "when the scorpion does not die?"

Hubert stepped on it, pressing hard.

Richard Lionheart went forth from his tent.

The king looked up at the sky, as though he had commanded it to stay where it was, and he looked at the earth, as though he had likewise ordered it to remain. He gave a nod—all was as it should be. The sight of him quickened some confidence in me I had not been aware of lacking.

He reviewed the horses, hoof and bridle, and the ostlers, the axelwrights and the joiners. He sifted the dwindling bread flour through his fingers, and examined the heap of sling stones with which the city had peppered us. A Saracen envoy had been skinned one night, long before our arrival, and his hide was stretched out, leathery and monstrous, on a frame of wood. King Richard stood before this ornament and mocked it in Frankish.

All the camp chuckled when they heard of this interview between the envoy's hide and the King of England. "Feeling hungry for a taste of pork, Sir Skin?" he said.

Something about King Richard lightened men's hearts, and made the songs more tuneful.

"Feeling well this morning, Sir Turd?" Hubert laughed, wiping his shoe.

The crack in the wall widened, and other cracks, like tributaries to a river, stretched out on either side. A faint chime reached our ears—chisels, masons feverish, fitting new stones. The sound recalled my boyhood, carters unloading bluestone while the mason's apprentices climbed the castle scaffold.

King Richard observed the catapults at work, and pointed out weak places that could be further punished. The wall broke into sections that crumbled like bread crust, but did not fall. Each blow fragmented an already broken wall, and the men of Acre no longer poured sand and mortar into the fissures.

As King Richard returned from inspecting the crossbowmen, his glance fell upon me, exercising the hammer, swinging it around my head. I was embarrassed to be seen wielding such a lowly weapon, but the king made a comment and his men smiled and nodded in my direction.

The good wines were gone, and even Sir Nigel had to be satisfied with thin, yellow stuff from Malta, and a sick-sweet drink from Samos. The Templar bread was richer than ever with baked weevils, their golden husks like seed. The whippet had vanished, and one of the king's men said he would cut off the right arm of the man who sliced his prize bitch into a saucepan.

But there was no whippet-stew—not in our tent. We had no meat, except for an occasional leathery horse steak. It's too bad, said Nigel, that horses can't feed on flies.

Sometimes at night the sentry's challenge woke me, and the next morning we would hear the news—we had captured more deserters from Acre.

Emissaries from our army, a Templar, and three of Richard's men, rode forth under a fluttering gold-and-scarlet flag of Saint George. They vanished into the Saracen camp that blocked the horizon to the east.

Soon all this would be over, our army camp believed—surely the siege would break. "They will not talk," said Hubert, "and make war at the same time."

When Wenstan sang while the parley was underway, his song was about the River Exe, how beautiful it flowed.

The emissaries rode back through a sea of mirage. They were carrying something, but we could not make out what. As they approached it was clear that they returned carrying dishes shrouded in silk brocade. When the silver platters were uncovered we marveled at the heaps of ice, the peaches and plums.

"Snow," said Nigel, "from Mount Hermon."

King Richard shared the fruit with King Philip, the Duke of Burgundy, and Guy de Renne, and with his own personal guard. These men ate the fruit, the juice running down their chins, laughing like boys.

A steward to the king passed to a chosen few, handing out a fistful of the pure snow. Rannulf was offered a handful, and he touched it to his face, cautious, like most fighting men, about washing with any variety of water. He offered me a remnant of glistening ice, and I accepted with surprise and gratitude.

"Saladin has refused to meet with King Richard," said Rannulf. "He says it is unwise for leaders to confer before a battle."

I felt a thrill at this news, the snow already so much water on my hands. The presence of King Richard meant that real battle would begin soon, and the prospect caused me much less dismay now. My master Otto had said that some men are so lucky that good fortune sweats out of them, through their pores. In a battle we would all want to ride near the king, and follow him.

The catapults went to work again, and I helped Rannulf into his mail shirt, buckled his belt, and gave his helmet a final polish.

"This will be no game for a swordsman," said Nigel, looking on. "Killing hungry men should not be difficult," he said. "But when you line up your best men, and ride hard into your enemy's best—that's a real pleasure, Edmund, and I pray we live to see it."

My own armor was more complete, now, a heavy chain mail skirt down to my knees.

A single swallow darted and circled. The sky was blue and empty.

Trumpets sounded, bleating, the horners dry mouthed. I gripped my hammer, and we took our places in the line of battle.

The bare ground before us winked and shimmered with mirage, and the city floated, shivering in the great round heat of the sky. An English standard-bearer collapsed, and his companions were quick to keep the battle flag from dipping. His squire pulled him from the line, and I sensed the impatience of the knights, even more than the pikemen, forced to face battle on foot.

Black birds with broad wings circled high above. When I touched the iron bands of my helmet, my fingers burned.

A roar, and a crash of iron against leather, and word traveled down the line: skirmishers from Saladin were attacking our flank. A shock rumbled through the army, shield jostling shield.

"They want to distract us," said Nigel. He gave a dry laugh, like a cough. "And they are doing a fair job of it."

The catapults worked without ceasing.

When the wall collapsed it was a great book falling open, with the satisfying rumble of new vellum. Dust ascended. A pagan army was exposed, tiny men, fine glittering swords.

Stay still, came the command.

Wait.

A goatskin sloshed from man to man, and I drank my share of acid wine. The command traveled down our battle front, a Frankish order, but I knew what it meant. We would stand forward when the king did, and not before.

King Richard took the lead, a stumbling, uneven line of knights under the heavy sun.

chapter
TWENTY-NINE

If there was a battle cry, I could not distinguish it from all the other human tumult.

The pagan army poured through the rubble. Our knights collided with them, and the battle looked already won, our fighting men with huge square bucklers, against their small, round target-shields.

The lightly armored Saracens went down, reeds before a flood. Steel flashed pink and scarlet.

Hubert and I were in the second wave of the attack, immediately following the knights. Already Rannulf and Nigel were lost in the flood of mail and helmets, surging into the multicolored pagans, pushing them back. Stones crashed into the knights from above. We raised our shields, the bucklers clattering, edges overlapping.

A blizzard swept us—arrows, lead darts, spears and spearheads, pebbles and bricks. The wreckage of a city poured into us, lintel shelves, broken urns, and huge, chisel-finished corner stones. Burning embers and sizzling coals darkened the air. Our army was forced together, breath crushed from lungs. We could not go forward; we could not turn back.

I stood on something pillow soft, and looked down to see a bright blue blouse, and a beard and earring, gleaming teeth. Before I could see if the man was alive, wounded or stunned, the army surged forward. I told myself I did not hear a dozen feet crushing the blue blouse into the earth.

The knight ahead of me was held erect by the crush of men, fluid trickling from inside his helmet. We climbed over a mountain of rubble, slipping, clambering, the stones jagged, the sunlight blinding.

My past, my future, consisted of this breathless climb. The rocks were slippery with red soup and broken teeth. I heard—or sensed—a cry, and reached back to offer Hubert the head of my hammer. He gripped the iron, and I pulled him up and over a jagged chunk of black rock.

Crusader knights slashed with the swords, each Christian struggling to win a space. The real danger was from the flanks, arrows and quarrels ripping the wool tunics that covered our mail.

Rannulf cut a Saracen giant across the face. All along the line Christian knights crumpled as bricks the size of Easter loaves crushed a shoulder, flattened a helmet.

The only battle cry I could discern was the high-pitched ululation of the Mussulmen. The crescent swords carved pieces from the wounded knights who stumbled into their line.

A signal passed through the defenders. One moment they fought cautiously, loathe to counterattack. And then they rushed forward, into us.

I struck a brilliant red shield with my hammer, brought down a Saracen, and before I could hesitate I kicked him, bellowing and digging hard with my foot.

Hubert struck a scimitar from a fist with his broadsword, but he slipped on a smear of blood. I stood before him, shielding Hu-

149

bert with my body. I was yelling wordlessly, the sound tearing my throat. I punched at Hubert's assailant with the head of my hammer, and the man flailed with his crescent sword. I punched him in the beard with my weapon, and he fell back.

Someone sliced the chain mail of my collar, the steel grating against the iron links. The force of the blow was so strong color left my vision, all the blood and the battle flags gray in an instant.

The taste in my mouth was gall—my liver, the organ of courage, filling me with anger. I heaved my shield upward to fend another blow. My assailant squinted with the strain of delivering another blow, a man with a henna-red beard. He shifted his attack, lunging at my face, at my eyes. I lifted my hammer.

I brought it down with my full strength, and the man was gone.

chapter
THIRTY

Quiet.

The city of Acre was a half hidden by yellow smoke.

Not only this place, this rubble-pocked field, was silent. The entire earth was stunned.

Not perfect silence—a fly buzzed, stuck in a wine jug. A Breton man-at-arms was whispering into the ear of a priest.

Hours had passed. Our army had retreated, and the Saracens had followed. Our pikemen had stiffened into a line, and they had torn into the Saracens in their exposed position, outside the walls. Our bowmen had emptied their quivers. When the pagans, in turn, retreated, taunting, not one of us had fallen into the trap.

So long ago.

I moved my arms, lifted my head, slowly. I drank from a brown, cord-bound gourd, water laced with wine. I was breathless, and could not drink any more. I was splayed out on the ground, unable to move my legs. Each breath was acrid, a lungful of dust. Coughing took too much strength.

An army was lying around me, thousands of men twitching like the mortally wounded. Water-bearers worked among us, and pleasure women sought out their favorites, bathing foreheads with water-and-vinegar-soaked rags.

The city of Acre was as it always had been, the gash in its wall barely visible through the haze. The ground between us and the walls was thick with bodies and torn armor.

Large black birds scattered across the battlefield, and Saracens and Christians searched among the dead, crying out when another breathing man was discovered. Armorers and their apprentices hunted, working their way through the mass of scattered war-stuff.

A man crouched beside me. The knight's dark mail was white with dust. He was bearded, his lips disfigured with a blue scar.

"Edmund?" Rannulf rasped.

"My lord," I whispered.

Rannulf called to a serving woman, and she hurried with a sloshing leather bottle of vinegar. Rannulf squeezed a cloth, and wiped my face.

I tried to protest, but he told me to keep my tongue silent in my mouth.

Another caked, grimy figure approached and knelt.

"You knocked the arm half off that infidel, Edmund," said Hubert's hoarse voice. "Smashed the bone!"

I made a very dry, creaking sound with my voice.

Hubert was all but unrecognizable, his face a mask of wall dust and ash. I coughed. "Did they hurt you, Hubert?" I heard my voice ask.

Hubert laughed wearily. He sounded old, ancient. "No," said Hubert, raggedly. For long time he did not speak again. "I fought hard, and I wounded one or two men."

I nearly said something to Rannulf, but the knight rocked his eyes toward Hubert and back to me. He gave a little shake of his head.

A stranger hobbled over, his face dark as a chestnut. "They want a parley," said Nigel's croak.

A small troop of Saracen warriors stepped carefully through the rubble, waving a pale blue banner, like house stewards bringing home a sheet of windblown laundry.

"How did you manage to find sword room," Rannulf was asking Nigel. "Thrust and ward-off, in such a crowd?"

Nigel said, "It was a mistake to try. I did more gouging and elbowing than cutting."

Servants worked the battlefield like serfs at harvest as the council took place in the cleared battlefield, under a wine-red canopy. Sir Guy de Renne sat cross-legged beside one of the pagan deserters from the city. The pagan leaned forward, one hand out, in the time honored pose of the interpreter. The evening grew heavy. Soon illumination was required, smoking lamps that flickered and sizzled, with the smell of olive oil.

Hubert cried out during the night, and I reached over to shake his shoulder. He sat up straight, swinging his arm wildly, staring around at the interior of the tent. When I spoke he did not hear me.

I did not dream.

The parley went on all night, but by morning, the meeting paused. The canopy fluttered in the weak wind, a luxurious covering, with sun-yellow fringe, large, harvest-auburn pillows on the ground. The battlefield was clear now, entirely stripped, and only a sole dog grazed the empty land.

The dog watched suspiciously, tail wagging very slightly as our camp stirred. A single bowman without mail or helmet, tousle haired and limping, was ordered out into the field, and the bowman made short work of nocking an arrow, and bringing the dog down. The day before there would have been cheers or laughter, but now no one made a sound.

Nigel spread a cloth dyed a rich, indigo blue. No English dyer could match such a dark hue, and no seamstress could have applied such perfect white tassel all the way around the border.

"Gifts from the people of Acre," said Nigel. "Isn't it wonderful that they feel so generous!" he added with an irony that sounded close to sympathy.

Sunlight winked off a finger ring, green jasper, excellent workmanship. Gold and fine silver gleamed among the colorful collection of anklets and head cloths. Copper abounded, too, and a bastard alloy of tin and silver, rings and bracelets that were pretty to the eye.

Sir Guy de Renne resumed his place under the canopy, and a Templar sat beside him. The emissaries from the city joined them, and even at this distance it was plain that Sir Guy de Renne was receiving them on behalf of King Richard and the noblemen.

Ships arrived, more wheat from Genoa, goats bleating, hens scratching the confines of their cages. Men rolled casks of red wine up the beach, the barrel staves seeping. Smiths worked in blue smoke, mending shattered sword blades, fitting new steel into hilts.

King Richard strode among us, quaffing wine from a goblet set with beryl and small rubies—showy stones, worth a knight's ransom, but what my master Otto would have called "poor to hand." I wished I could work a cup for the king, forge it, and set it on his table.

Every Christian had buckets of wine while the parley continued. Horse-leather buckets, goatskin sacks, bronze pails, pink gourds, every imaginable container filled to overflowing with red, and emptied down Crusader gullets. Men fell flat out, half slain by the heat and the new drink. White hen feathers drifted in the hot wind. At first a chorus of goats and lambs bleated. The livestock cry was decimated, then halved, then diminished to a few, querying bleats. And then the last kids were silent. Cooking smoke rose over the camp.

Men ate without speaking. They sucked hot fat from their fingers. Men gave themselves to goat steaks and lamb legs, closing their eyes, stopping only to drink more wine, the red liquid pattering on the ground. There was a trance-like frenzy about the feeding pikemen.

As I sat, my belly full, I felt a step beside me. It was Father Urbino, looking thin and sunburned, his eyelashes white with dust.

The priest put a hand on my arm.

"You help to kill the enemies of our Lord," he said, in his heavy Paduan accent.

I nodded.

"Be happy, Edmund!" he said with a smile.

I assured myself that I was too weary to have any feelings, and if I let myself picture a trampled body, a splash of blood, I pushed the image from my mind—perhaps because I sensed I would see worse.

chapter
THIRTY-ONE

At a distance the sound of skirmishing was the much like sound of boys roughhousing in a brook—the churn of stones, the excited cries, the jeers.

A leather shield clashed with a war hammer, and broke. A horse received the shock of a brace of crossbow quarrels with a sound like a bellows, all the air in his body released in one great shudder.

As the harriers from Saladin's army worried our sentries, the Duke of Burgundy's falconer lost an arm, shaved clean with a stroke of Damascus steel. A few pikemen gut-wounded the pagan attacker's steed, although the heathen knight himself escaped on foot. One of the duke's men carried the severed arm wrapped in vermilion silk.

The parley before the city continued despite the efforts of Saladin to distract both the city fathers of Acre and the Christian army. Sir Guy de Renne could be seen bending forward, gesturing grandly. Nearly all the envoys leaned on pillows, exhausted or at peace. Christian stewards entered the city with pack horses, and some of King Richard's staff could be seen on the city walls, surveying, making lists. Pack horses left the city gates, heavy laden with loads wrapped in richly colored carpets.

One of the carrion birds descended to meet his own shadow not far from the parley, and when he touched earth took a moment to fold his wings.

The bird flew at last, just off the ground, and then banked, spiraling majestically over the gray rubble of the city walls, throwing a shadow over the parley-canopy. A Saracen bowman stepped from the canopy shadow, and fingered resin over his bowstring. A quiet word from a Saracen chief, and the arrow returned to its quiver, the bird unharmed.

Nigel was careful to shave each morning, with a razor of Cordovan steel, peering into his shiny metal mirror. He rubbed his cheeks with essence of rose, and wore sleeves of brushed fine wool, sky blue. His town-grimy appearance was forgotten now that we were at war, and even though Rannulf was careless regarding his hair and beard, his chain mail gleamed.

When Rannulf beckoned for me to follow him, I did, and Rannulf passed easily through the king's men, spoke with a Breton guard in a slurred a half Frankish, half English, and entered one of the counting tents.

"The treasure of Acre," said Rannulf. Guards, tall men with handsome, butter-blond leather belts, and gold fittings, nodded to my knight.

Rannulf picked up a leather helmet, set with pink-hued pearls. I examined an amulet interlocking gold inlaid with blackest enamel. Each spur, each silver bridal necklace was a dowry prize or some virgin's gift from her mother. Even a pair of shoes was cunning, fine leather, so supple it hung from my hand like silk.

"We make an inventory," said the king's chamberlain in stiff, oblong English. "Every household, every lord and maiden in

157

Acre, must empty every coffer. The lord king does not desire to be cheated."

Chamberlain's servants sorted the leather from the silk, the stone-inlaid from the unadorned. More carpets heavy with riches arrived, and were dumped on the growing array of weapons and plate, clothing and jewels.

"These are rare gems," said Rannulf in a low voice.

"My master Otto was an expert at such things. That quail's egg made of green glazing is an emerald, or I'm a heathen. That is amethyst," I said, indicating a bracelet set with lavender jewels.

"They come from the Far East," said Rannulf.

"And this glass, starlike stone. I cannot guess its name—"

"A diamond," said Rannulf. He pronounced it *diamant*. "I saw such once in my life, on the finger of a Moorish knight at a great tournament in Provence. An unexampled thing is hard to value. I must think of some worthy advice to offer the king, or he will melt down all this finery in a great pot, and pour it into ingots."

"That would be a sin!" I gasped.

"Oh, King Richard is a great sinner," said Rannulf.

chapter
THIRTY-TWO

The prisoners arrived.

The entire garrison, and most of Acre's inhabitants, emptied into our camp. Stripped of their multicolored clothing, their head cloths and their sword belts, they looked diminished, their faces pinched with hunger. These fighting men were reduced to a long, creeping line of ordinary humans, silent, eyes to the ground. Some of the men had families, women huddled close to their men, children dull-eyed and silent.

Following the orders of their own marshals these warriors filed into a field between our camp and the beach. The area had been cleared with difficulty, and several men in priestly raiment argued with the king's guard, annoyed that their tent pegs had to be uprooted. They were forced to move to a remote corner of the camp, their reasoning went, so "this army of Christ-offending rats" would have a safe place to set their haunches.

Pikemen looked on, in full agreement with the priests, spitting and muttering curses.

Nigel watched as the shuffling defenders of Acre sat, shoulder to shoulder. An infant began to wail.

"How will they eat?" said Hubert.

"Through their teeth," said Nigel, "in the same manner as you and I."

I entered the city through the great main gate, Hubert at my side. The gash in the walls, the heap of fractured stone, were all the more ruinous viewed from within.

The castle of Acre had been built by the Franks after the early Crusades, decades before my birth. The capture of this noble citadel by the heathen had been bitter news in the guildhalls of Christendom. The gloried domes and archways of the fortifications struck me dumb, the scars of swallows' nests stippling the inner curve of the domes high above. The holy sanctuaries had been sown with wool carpets, and festooned with gold-leaf symbols of pagan faith.

Christian priests and their men labored even now to unload the churches of this insult, carpets rolled up, and clean straw rushes strewn about. A Latin prayer drifted through the alternating sun and shadow, ardent *in nomines* driving the Devil from the naves. Frankincense perfumed the air.

The side streets were denuded, every latchstring and window curtain of a groat's worth having long since been taken. Up some stone-paved lanes Frankish squires and footmen were celebrating, bare haunches rutting on the thin, splayed forms of pagan women.

If this sight shocked me for an instant I quickened my pace. The dead were arranged in the deep shade of a side street. A woman in a dark shawl looked up at us, her face tear-stained. She cursed us—there was no mistaking her message.

Hubert was trailing behind, not paying the woman any mind. He picked up a stone absentmindedly, a pretty thing, half quartz, which had probably been used to dress some wealthy man's dwelling. I could see the stages of Hubert's impulses, free to throw the stone in any direction, at any material or living thing. Or to keep it. The woman's voice interrupted Hubert's thoughts, challenging him to go ahead and knock her on the head with the rock.

Hubert put the stone down gently. "A right proud city," said Hubert, ignoring the woman following us, screeching, weeping. We both made a show of ignoring her, climbing stars, hurrying along battlements, ascending towers, until we could not hear her cry.

The sea breeze from the top of the walls was sweet with salt. Galleys lined the harbor protectively, pennons fluttering, the scarlet-and-gold silk of Saint George or the blue, flowering lozenge of the Plantagenets. When I saw our camp, flags and peaked tents, the distant figures of Christian folk, I was swept with pride. How had the heathen dared to stand in our way?

Far to the east, Saladin brooded with his army. Word was that Saladin had been surprised at the fall of Acre, aware too late that he should have acted in force. Rannulf believed that Saladin would honor the surrender agreement, but join battle when he thought we could be crushed.

Dreaminess descended upon us again.

The heat filled the space around every man and every horse. Hubert and I spent time searching for shade among the tents, along the granary, the diminishing sacks of oats and bundles of hay.

Hubert was withdrawn, despite all I could do to distract him. I tried to bet him a button that one ant would beat another to the ant hole, or that Nigel would laugh before Rannulf would spit. Hubert thanked me for my effort in a gentle voice, but said that gambling was, after all, forbidden.

King Philip of France left the camp, borne by stewards and chamberlains. His fever had turned his skin yellow, and the hand he raised in valediction to us all was greenish in the sunlight.

"Of course he's green," said Nigel. "He has all the courage of a toad!"

Most of the Francomen remained, including one duke called Conrad, who claimed a corner of the city from the Templars. A group of Breton knights threw a battle standard into a ditch near the city walls, insulting the men of Anjou. The troops of Guienne quarreled with the soldiers of Lusignan, something to do with a woman. Quarrels broke out among every order of knight and man, clerk and chamber boy.

The hard-working bakers no longer filled our bellies with warm white flour cakes. Their broad wooden paddles brought loaves of maslin-bread from their domed, clay ovens. The loaves were like the earth-dark bread of the poorest peasants. Our prisoners ate horse cakes, bran and straw, the sort beasts of burden feed on.

The prisoners numbered two thousand seven hundred mouths. They accepted their defeat with no sound of complaint, waiting for the parleys that would agree on the price that would return them to their families and friends. The first emissaries rode out from Saladin's camp, horsemen with silk and black leather armor, highly burnished appointments, studs and pommels.

An innkeeper-turned-soldier was caught with a pair of ox-bone dice, swore he was holding them for a friend he would not incriminate, and the entire army stood watch as a muscular summoner from Ghent gave him ten lashes with a whip. The Templars and the Hospitallers took quarters in the city, as did many other hand-picked troops. While that gave us more space, it did nothing to enrich our stores of food, and left Guy de Renne to police an army of former harvesters and woodsmen with a small corps of seasoned knights.

Sir Nigel and Rannulf made much of their experience with men, striding through the blizzard of flies to order new latrines to be dug, but the Duke of Burgundy and King Richard took to their tents, and day by day the heat grew worse.

The prisoners began to expire, their brothers-in-arms keening softly over their remains. The sight won little sympathy from most pikemen, who prayed for the hour all Mussulmen would swallow their tongues.

chapter
THIRTY-THREE

The day began with a cool, gentle wind, and with the feeding and exercising of the chargers.

Then came the heat again, and the low-voiced final rites for the latest to die of fever, and an early afternoon meal of horse-meat and chaff bread.

Two pleasure women got into a fight over a pearl earring, a tearing, howling battle, and barely a voice was raised in cheer or derision. The women tore at each other's hair and eyes, grew tired, dropped panting. The sentries prodded them with the staffs of their halberds, and they moved on.

The priests kept their prayer hours, and we joined them. The last wine turned to vinegar in the cup, and the guards slept standing up, leaning into their staves.

"I would fall down, if I tried it," said Hubert. "As soon as I began to snore." He did an instantaneous imitation of a sleeping guard pitching forward, fast asleep. He caught himself just before he landed on his face.

"It is the result of much art," I said, pleased to see Hubert in good humor again. "You and I have yet to learn to sleep like fighting men."

When King Richard strode from his tent that afternoon, the camp stirred, neighbor nudging neighbor. King Richard was in dress armor, the brightest mail, an indigo cape flowing nearly to the ground. The king, accompanied by his personal guards and Sir Guy de Renne, hurried over to the roped-off area where the prisoners hunched, heads down, twenty-seven hundred humans as quiet as sweltering beasts.

The camp was rising to its feet, man and knight, waterboy and fletcher, all wondering what could bring a monarch into such heavy sunlight, through the thick black flies. Richard reached to his belt, pulled out a bright broadsword, and sawed briefly at the hairy, taut hemp rope that marked the prisoners' frontier.

Cut through, the cord fell hard, lifting curls of dust. The rope barrier slumped around the circumference of the prisoner herd. Foot soldiers seized their pikes. Yeoman soldiers picked up their axes. Men crowded close. A few of the knights loosened the blades in their scabbards, the camp intent on the king.

King Richard said, "All of them."

Les tout.

And he made the unmistakable gesture, a finger across his throat.

Sir Guy de Renne hesitated for the briefest moment, making a show of freeing his own sword, turning to locate his clerks. Perhaps he was giving King Richard time to make his order more clear, or to amend it.

The king said, "Now!"

Sir Guy de Renne set his feet, like a man about to receive a blow, and caught the eye of Nigel and Rannulf. The two English knights looked on with no expression in their eyes. Sir Guy called for his chief clerk, an assistant with a leather pipe-roll crammed with scrolls. He completed the act of drawing his blade, and gave an order to the chief pikeman.

There was a space of time, three heartbeats, when nothing happened.

The first blow sent a wave through the prisoners, a gasp like a great wind. A few of the men struggled to rise, but the tethers around their hands and feet hobbled them, and they fell. A woman began to plead. The prisoners swarmed in place, trapped.

A child bawled, a noise like a crippled calf I had heard once, its hindquarters torn by foxes. The male prisoners cried out, one or two quick-thinking enough to argue in their incomprehensible tongue.

The pikeman did not hesitate, but some of the swordsmen looked back at the king, at Sir Guy de Renne, and then returned to their work.

Hubert called out, tried to arrest a pikeman hurrying to the butchery, and I had to drag Hubert away.

I kept Hubert from seeing it, held his face away from the sight, although the sloppy crunch of blade and ax, and the smell of blood and fresh-torn bowels could not be ignored. Or the cries of Christians calling out saint's names, Saint George who slew the winged serpent, and the giant Saint Christopher who carried Our Lord across a wide river. A sword makes a butcher-shop whine across the bones and sinews of a neck.

The calls of the still-living prisoners must have reached the outriders, because soon an irregular attack streamed across the plain from Saladin's camp. Our bowmen made easy work of keeping them at a distance.

A voice called out that each heathen killed was one less enemy to God. It was Father Urbino, his blond hair dark with sweat. He shook his fist, urging the pikemen at their labor.

Many knights did not enter the harvest. The few Templar men present turned away and left the rest to their work. Nigel watched with a stony gaze. When I caught his eye he let his expression shift to one of stoic distaste. When the tide of fly-carpeted blood crept close to us, Nigel kicked up a dike of dust to keep it from our feet.

But many knights labored beside the pikeman, and many English knights, too. Rannulf grew tired of watching hackwork, and made his way through the scarlet-soaked corpses, and demonstrated a sword stroke, severing first one life, then another, each death quick. He quit the field, shaking his head.

Nigel and Rannulf stood beside each other, arms folded, and only moved when the red tide crept too close.

chapter
THIRTY-FOUR

It was twilight.

A cool wind from the sea blew among the tents. It fluttered the pennons and standards overhead, a loud, percussive sound.

We could still nose the smell of slaughter, just a few hours ago.

Hubert and I had wandered to the edge of the camp, where the beach was guarded by a few Corsican spear-bearers, small, quick men who called out to each other jokingly, "Who goes there?" "Name yourself!" and many such things in their jaunty tongue.

The sea breeze was delicious. Crusader galleys and sailing ships clawed off, away from the shore, finding new anchorage in the distance. Saracen warships skulked, furtive beetles on the horizon.

"None of this——" Hubert began, and then fell silent.

I waited, feeling incapable of offering him consolation.

"Nothing is what I expected," said Hubert at last.

One of the Corsican spearmen challenged us, in accent-warped English, mock-English, really, because many of the soldiers found the sound of our language amusing. "Password, if you please."

Hubert did not seem to hear the little man.

"Password, English," said the brightly garbed sentries, all red stripes and silk leggings.

Hubert looked at him without much show of interest.

"Identify, squire," said the Corsican.

Hubert stared, his glance something close to insolence.

The sentry rose to his toes, sticking out his neck, uttering a stream of Corsican curses and challenges.

Hubert put his hands around the sentry's neck, and shook the man's head on its stalk.

Sentries came running, tired of watching the choppy surf, as I stepped between the two.

I gave a little speech, in Frankish, English, and as much Latin as I could squirrel out of my memory. We didn't know the password, I tried to explain, but were pleased that the sentries were taking such strong precautions.

I wished them all well, thanked them for their patience, and kept a strong grip on Hubert's collar all the way back to Sir Nigel's tent.

Sir Nigel exploded. "I forbid it!"

"I will return to England," insisted Hubert. "My father will pay you in gold for my passage."

"He can pay me in pickled testicles!" said Nigel. "You stay with me."

Hubert began to say more, but Nigel cut him off with a gesture.

The two were quiet, Hubert steadfastly waiting in the center of the tent, Nigel pacing from one corner to another. The tent was large, shifting subtly with the wind outside. The tent ropes hummed with the breeze, and sand hissed quietly against the canvas. Wenstan polished Sir Nigel's shield, working intently, as though none of us were present.

The candlelight simmered. "Did you think it would be easy?" Nigel said at last. "Did you think it would be a game for boys, wooden swords and warriors stuffed with hay?"

Hubert stood still, and only now did I let myself experience the shame—I had stood by while good men scythed the heathen, and I had done nothing to help. Sir Nigel could indulge himself, believing, apparently, that he should not blacken his sword on a woman. But I had betrayed my king, and, I began to believe, Heaven.

"Do you think I've been joyful every day," continued Nigel, "in this dry hole? But I have done my duty, Hubert, before God."

The candles fluttered and nearly went out. The tent flap opened, and Rannulf entered the light.

"Hubert is going home, my lord," I told Rannulf in a whisper.

"And you, Edmund, have no doubt poured ideas into Hubert's head," said Nigel.

I kept silent.

"Your Edmund displeases me, Rannulf," said Nigel. "He needs scoring with an ox whip, or I am a witch."

Rannulf wore the expression of a man very sorry he had come in out of the night. He began to speak, but did not have the chance to make a sound.

"I am thirty-seven years old," said Nigel. "And tired in my marrow. Who knows how many more years God will grant me? I am not an abbot or a priest—I've always envied those godly men of books, each morning winning Heaven's ear with a prayer. It's so easy for those gentlefolk. I am an ordinary fighting man,

Hubert. A worthless man—and I have been called to wear my shield for the Queen of Heaven."

Hubert took a deep breath, and let it out slowly.

Rannulf was standing the way men do when they are full of news. He had said nothing critical of my refusal to join in the slaughter, but Rannulf was one of those who make others guess his thoughts.

"What is it, Rannulf? What has our wise lord king decided now?" barked Nigel. "Maybe there is a girl's choir he would like us to carve into chops."

Rannulf took his time, now that he had Nigel's ear. He found his cup, sipped carefully through his scarred lips, and said, "We are breaking camp."

"You are not funny, Rannulf," said Nigel, kicking a wrinkle in the carpet.

"The order has already been given," said Rannulf. "All women are to leave the camp immediately."

Nigel gave a silent laugh, a throaty sound, shaking his head in disbelief. "We're taking to sea," he said. "We're following the Frankish king, like cowards. Like Hubert here. Retreating to our ships. Am I right?"

Rannulf gave us all a smile with his eyes. "We will march south, along the coast, and seek battle with Saladin's army." He relished his tidings, draining the last of his wine.

"Unless, of course," Rannulf added, "you prefer to stay here."

No one slept that night.

Looking like rabble, we worked, knight and man. The king's guard struck his tents and set up a spear wall around the royal baggage. Nigel ordered the ostlers to gird and saddle our horses.

Before dawn the carts were greased and loaded, horses pressed into service under bundles of tents and cords of tent pegs. Bowmen paced ahead to protect the landward flank of an army that already stretched south down the beach.

Donkeys were now a part of our army, odd, stumpy-legged animals. These beasts made wheezing, laughing complaints as the men packed them. As the entire army creaked south it looked like a crawling miracle. So much that had been inert and fetid was now on the move.

But so much was left behind, axles and crates, worn leather buckets and fittings, huge bonfires streaking flames and black smoke. Our siege engines had been broken into parts, and only some of the dismantled sections were loaded onto gray horses. Much was fed to the fires, including Sir Skin on his wooden frame.

The treasure had been broken up, stones pried from their settings, silver mauled and melted into bricks. Richard had given the orders that no pleasure women were to follow, and vicious arguments among the women greeted this news, women refusing to listen, spitting, cursing, and following the army in disregard to the king. Even the washerwomen were to be left behind, in theory. Rannulf said they would smell us in Jerusalem days before they saw us. The Burgundians said that they would slit their own throats rather than ride in squalor.

The king relented; washerwomen rejoiced. Pagan scouts rode under light guard, spearmen shielding them from revenge, and from any impulse to return to their brethren. The army made a churning chorus of groans and gristle, leg joints and phlegmy lungs of man and beast, making an impressive noise even from well ahead of the army, where Hubert and I rode the leading edge. He carried one of Nigel's battle lances, a fluttering scarlet pennon at the point.

Soon, the wind sang.

Soon Saladin's army would move to stop our progress, and there would be the great, open battle we had all dreamed about.

I was convinced that I longed for pitched battle as well as any man. Caught up in the hubbub of the march, I felt no fear.

Winter Star capered beneath me, kicking like a goat, my hammer sleeping heavily in its leather boot. Hubert's horse Shadow caught the mood, jigging and snorting, Hubert unable to keep from smiling at his steed's eagerness. But soon all the horses were shaking their manes, rolling eyes, even Sir Nigel having trouble gripping the bridle. Hubert and I steadied our horses while the knights and squires caught up with us. Sir Guy de Renne reined in his horse until the beast foamed at the bit.

"There's something troubling them," said Rannulf, a note of compassion in his voice.

"They act like they smell bear," said Nigel.

"Or lion," said Rannulf.

He took it upon himself to ride east, pausing for me to follow.

chapter
THIRTY-FIVE

The air was perfumed with spice, the sort sold to the richest ladies, pinch by pinch, on the spicer's scale.

"We march south, with the Infidel ships on our seaward side, the Saracen army between us and Jerusalem," said Rannulf. "How long do you think we will keep from starving?"

Late morning sun filled the grass, each shaft glittering. The dew was long since gone. We rested our hoses under the tall, plumed date palms, big fronds like huge brittle feathers under the horse's hooves.

"I know nothing of such strategy," I said at last.

Rannulf shook his head. "Counterfeit meekness, Edmund," he said. "Every man with a belly can think."

"I hope there will be a battle soon," I said.

"Do you?"

It was true enough, and I wanted to say so, but he stood tall in his stirrups, searching the ground, leaning against his hunting lance. He said, "If we found the track of a lion, and reported it, the king would be greatly pleased. It would help you win back his favor."

"Have I so badly lost our lord king's favor?" I heard myself ask.

"And counterfeit ignorance. Your prove a smooth liar, squire," he said, with something like gentleness. "You did not join in the general slaughter." He said this as easily as though he discussed a horse race.

"Many fighting men did not."

"And many did." To my surprise Rannulf shrugged. "Sometimes the sword will not leave the sheath."

"A squire lives for his master, and his master's lord," I responded, wondering if I should have assisted Rannulf in butchering the prisoners.

Rannulf said, "If we found a big cat's spoor and brought back its skin, the king would never forgive either of us."

Our own army trailed forever, and to the east a haze of white dust shadowed our forces. Saladin's men were not slow to parallel our path, his terraces of tents already vanished, the beautiful yellows and blues rolled up and gone.

"But think how every man and woman would admire us," I said.

The wind kicked up a flurry of empty dust. Far away, the troop of washerwomen trailed our army. I kept finding them with my eyes.

"We crave the admiration of women," Rannulf agreed, almost sadly. "Heaven makes them so alluring so we do not see their true nature."

"Is a woman's nature very different from a man's?"

"As unlike a man's as a leper is unlike Achilles. Why do you think King Richard prefers the company of young men?"

"I am so ignorant," I offered. So painfully unknowing, so forcibly chaste, I meant. So virginal, despite my longing.

"You are spared sorrow," said Rannulf. "The female soul is dwarfed and hideous, Edmund. If we could see through a woman's beautiful form, and see her inward nature, we would cringe with disgust. Praise Heaven that you have been spared a woman's touch."

Many Christian men felt as Rannulf did, but I certainly did not. I found myself with the ever-fresh memory of Elviva, her hand out to mine as I reached down to touch her in farewell.

Outriders approached, a thudding, shuffling gallop.

Winter Star shuddered, and I leaned forward, gripping his mane. Rannulf had trouble with his own mount.

Winter Star kicked sideways, trying to turn back.

"Camels," said Rannulf.

I had heard of the camel-leopard, a beast with spots and a huge body, who could call out with the voice of a beautiful woman. The firmament overlooked many such wonders: the griffin, half lion, half eagle, that guarded buried treasure; the harpy, half woman, half bird, who tormented travelers.

These loping, lurching steeds frightened me, even as a nervous laugh escaped my lips. The riders beat at the sides of these swollen creatures, and each camel stretched out its neck, opened a lipless mouth and gave a terrible bleat. Much slashing was required to motivate these camels toward us, heavy, pillowy hooves flopping on the hard ground as they came on.

Winter Star began to steady his nerve just as I was sure I had lost mine.

"Do camels eat human flesh?" I asked, trying to sound more courageous than I felt.

Rannulf took the question seriously, or pretended to. "I think they do not," he said.

"This is good news," I responded shakily.

Rannulf leveled his hunting lance, and nudged his mount forward a pace or two, as I followed.

The camel-riders yanked and sawed at the long necks of their monsters. They took a position a long bowshot from us, the camels bawling in complaint.

Squire duty required me to say, "My lord—you should take up your shield." It was held by its trappings to the saddle.

The outriders sang out a high, ululating cry.

Rannulf gave a toss of his lance, like a man distracted by children: *What are you waiting for?*

The camelmen showed their teeth, commenting among themselves, greatly amused. A rider with flowing sulfur-yellow sleeves pointed and his companions urged their bawling camels into new positions. The riders flicked their swords, brilliant crescents, and the leader gave a short challenge in a high, tenor voice.

"Should we take the lives of those camel-warriors?" Rannulf was asking, lightly, in great humor. "Or spare them?"

"My lord," I said, keeping my voice from trembling, "as you wish."

chapter
THIRTY-SIX

But the camelmen did not attack. At a signal from one, they all turned, their mounts grunting. They trotted away from us, beyond a lingering veil of dust.

When we were back at the verge of our army again, we encountered the king.

King Richard was on horseback. His hair flowed golden around his head. His thick neck and handsome square face were sunburned. A brace of bloody coneys dangled from his saddle, and his horse was black with sweat.

The king gestured with one of the dead rabbits, a stiff, big-eyed puppet. When one of the guard did not answer quickly enough, the king flung the bloody doll in the man's face.

The king's eyes showed Rannulf a flicker of respect, but he did not glance my way. He leaned forward to wave a fly from his quarry. He watched the tiny insect circle upward.

He snatched it, missed, and cursed. He made another grab.

He raised his fist, squeezing it hard, radiant. The men around him smiled, and visibly relaxed.

"Have you seen any lions on your ride into the hills?" King Richard asked Sir Rannulf.

"None but you, my lord king," said Rannulf.

Perhaps we had all assumed that the train of baggage and camp
followers would protect our rear. But each morning a raid cleared
away another few dozen washerwomen, who fled without resis-
tance.

Soon we began to lose horses, too.

Hordes of dark-skinned men attacked our rear. These fighters
were darker than black wine, and they swooped down on foot,
arms and ankles decorated with gold. They were joined by horsemen wearing long, flowing headgear, who cut at our rearguard
with lusty if inaccurate strokes.

The Templar knights had little trouble slicing these Bedouin attackers off their horses, but more raiders came down upon us to
take the place of the slain. Soon many of our veteran divisions were
repositioned in the rear to protect what was left of our provisions.

King Richard rode up and down the length of our entire
straggling line, and Wenstan sang the song of the knight before
the green river, pitying the enemy on the other side.

Each day was a flat, endless road of dust like powdered bone.
My mouth filled with stone mortar. We came upon our pagan
scouts, eyes and privy parts gouged, bellies swollen in the sun.
The heat was heavier than ever before, horses collapsing with ribs
heaving mightily, men fainting.

One advancing Burgundian knight pitched hard from his
mount, and before his squire could reach him a Bedouin on a
sleek, charcoal-dark horse, came from nowhere. He rode to
where the knight sprawled, and thrust a spear into his groin.

We groaned at the sight. The Bedouin called out, throwing
down his spear, making a show of spreading his arms: *Come and
get me.*

Our army shivered, a thrill of anger traveling the length of our long column, but Sir Guy de Renne and Sir Nigel called for us to stay as we were.

Hubert's eyebrows and lashes were white with dust, and he looked like an elderly uncle. "Soon," he said in a hoarse whisper, half encouragement, half prayer.

I nodded agreement, but I did not feel this confidence in my heart. We could plod along the coast forever, I believed. I conceived a grudging respect for Saladin, a commander with the sun and the hard blue sky fighting on his side.

Our progress halted near a place Nigel said was called Arsuf.

"The scouts have a name for every knoll," Wenstan said.

His manner had changed here in the Holy Land. His stammer was rare now, and his tread steady and calm. He looked years younger, too, not at all like Nigel and Rannulf, who had new, hard creases in their cheeks. I had heard him singing one of Miles's old ballads recently, the one about the gander's head caught in milady's bower.

"I have been talking to our infidel companions," he said. "If your horse makes water, the scouts later say, 'Ah, you remember when your horse wet upon the Rocky Place of the Stone Ginn.' A ginn, they tell me, is a spirit who lives inside a place."

A thrill swept me, that we rode through a land rich with devils. "What does 'Arsuf' mean, then?" I asked.

Wenstan squinted at the land around us. "Flat place, I would guess."

Hubert kicked Shadow into a shuffling gallop. His red pennon fluttered all the way up the ranks, and hurried back again.

He was too excited to answer when I asked him, but by then commands were being bawled in a dozen languages, troops form-

ing ranks, knights gathering, assembling in a ragged line, struggling into mail skirts and helmets.

I called for Rannulf, but in the cacophony of voices and
trumpets, I heard no answer. King Richard rode ahead, along
what had been the rear of our army but was now the rapidly
forming front. Sir Guy de Renne called orders in the rising dust.

At last Rannulf flung himself from his warhorse. Dust brought
tears to my eyes.

"Edmund," he said, "dress me for battle."

chapter
THIRTY-SEVEN

And still the fighting did not begin.

All morning horsemen drew our bow shots, arcing arrows that glinted in the sky. They rattled to the ground as the enemy cantered out of range. A playful, market-day quality about this made it look like sport. The camel riders were few, and they stayed well back.

The air was aromatic with the scent of mint, herbs trodden flat under our feet. Gradually, our bowmen began to conserve their arrows, and waterboys circulated with kidskins of water and wine. Some of the pikemen made a show of how much they could drink down without taking a breath. An emir, a pagan battle chief, paced his horse calmly, well within bow range, accompanied by his men.

"They're counting us," Hubert suggested.

"No, I don't think so," I said. The Saracens knew our number, I was sure, every ostler, every cook. The emir was taking his pleasure so close to danger, and letting us watch this demonstration of how brave he was.

The bulk of Saladin's manpower was screened by a stunted

ridge of evergreens in the distance, the trees swaying and shrugging with the passage of warriors. It was hardly a surprise when King Richard had us reform, marching us ahead to take a new position. We gazed across ground unmarred by a single hoof, pebbles glinting like coins.

The Templars, with their black-and-white shields, took the southern end of the line, nearest the sea. Frankish knights, Bretons and the men of Guienne, planted their feet beside them, blaspheming and outdoing themselves in taunts.

In the center of the line was the king, with his English pikemen, and his Norman foot soldiers. On the extreme left was a rank of Hospitallers, many of them kneeling in prayer. The king rode up and down the front, his horse's eyelashes heavy with dust.

We were beautiful—I had not expected this. All along the line, interspersed with the pike-bearers, were archers. Each archer hammered a *cheveux-de-frix* into the ground, a picket of sharpened staves, behind which he took his position. Bowmen, I knew from my boyhood, generally spend a good deal of time fussing with their arrow feathers, rubbing beeswax on their bowstrings. These archers were no different, flexing their shoulders, sharing pinches of resin and plucking tufts of weeds from underfoot. Crossbowmen assembled with them, counting out their quarrels.

And still—no bloodshed.

Wearing chain mail and wool is like being a much stouter, slower moving man, each crook of the arm causing the mail to pinch, or to ripple with a subtle, metallic slither. With this addition of weight came an emotional stolidity, too, a sense of being committed to the strength of one's horse, and the skill of the mailsmith.

Even so, I would have paid any amount in silver to have this over and done. Rannulf wrested the helmet from his head. He ran his tongue over his scarred lips. I could see the fear in his eyes—not a fear of blood, but anxiety that nothing would happen.

"Surely we can't all wait forever," I offered. The truth was that now, with battle so close, much of my old fear of fighting was continuing to stir.

"I pray not, Edmund," he said.

I longed to see nightfall.

One moment we were a force of sweating men, joking that Saladin had an army of whoremongers. We itched and sneezed with the rising dust, and adjusted each others belts, easing the weight of hot mail on shoulders.

And then the day changed.

Thousands of dark-skinned men streamed at us from the woods. These warriors wore no armor. They came fast, carrying spears and small targets. The attackers screamed with a noise so shrill that our horses stirred at the sound. I could not quite believe that this was battle at last. The dark, sweaty men seemed like celebrants of a festival.

Our archers were quick to bend their bows, and the crossbowmen joined them, but the shower of arrows did nothing to slow the assault. The exuberance of the attack made this all seem like a frenzied May Day romp, no one likely to be hurt. The pointed staves were wrenched aside, and the bowman forced to rush back behind the lines.

And yet it was like a midsummer tussle among apprentices, no blood. Our foot soldiers were rocked, startled by the quickness of these dark men, and by the Bedouin runners who joined them, cutting and stabbing. Men began to fall.

Our knights stayed on horseback, refusing to join the foot soldiers, and Hubert and I hunched forward on our mounts, too, enduring the storm, letting our pikemen counterstroke these assailants. Pikestaffs made a loud clatter, and when a footman near me was struck hard he gasped, like a wrestler whose wind has been slammed from his body.

The pikemen retreated slowly, and there was no festive air in the way they lunged and wrestled, giving way step by step, until the line was maintained only by the hedge of horsemen, Hubert and I among them.

Winter Star trembled under the onslaught of howling warriors. I clubbed awkwardly with my hammer, sometimes smashing a leather-and-star target with one blow, but often missing. Hubert laid about him with his sword.

Several times Winter Star lurched and groaned, and I nearly reeled from my mount. But a war saddle is fitted with a pommel that juts up before the rider, a bright, brass knob. I put this pommel to good use, hooking it with my thigh when I felt myself about to tumble.

I paid little attention to the blows, although they hurt, until I saw the blond shafts of spears on the ground. I realized without an instant of anxiety that I was being struck with these missiles, the points blocked by my wool tunic, with its Crusader star, my mail, and my thick wool undercoat. A spear glanced off Winter Star's right flank, but the warhorse remained steady.

My duty was to see that Rannulf's lance neither fell nor shattered, to make sure he kept to his saddle. The line of armored horsemen took never so much as a step backward, holding from north to south. The knights were full helmeted, and bent forward into the hail of spears, while the squires were less well protected. A few of these youths lost their mounts, and were lost in the stew of fighting men.

In an instant, the dark-skinned men broke, running away. But as they retreated, the pagan horsemen attacked, thundering through the fleeing footmen.

chapter
THIRTY-EIGHT

I was wedged in by a crush of horses and knights, and could not lift my hammer. I felt panic of frustration, and warded off blows with my shield. This sick fear ripened into anger. These strangers were trying to gash and lance my body.

I wrenched my hammer free, ready to help my friend. Hubert engaged a pagan knight, a warrior with thick jowls. This Infidel wore no helmet, his face exposed. He grinned painfully under the rain of Hubert's blows. The man parried with an ax polished to a gleam, but Hubert was intent, thrashing with his sword as slices of white appeared on the man's head and face. The white cuts welled immediately with red, and blood traveled down his shoulder. The man's head half parted from his body, and the warrior dropped.

Hubert's face was pale, his mouth set, as we turned our attention to the other riders, coming on hard. And then, at some signal only they could see, the horsemen wheeled and departed, racing away behind the chalky haze.

The wind rippled the manes of our horses and fluttered the battle standards. Dust cleared. A horse far down the line was screaming.

"Let us go after them!" cried Sir Nigel through the slits of his helmet. He sounded like a man yelling from inside a tub. King Richard rode hard up and down the wall of men, commanding us to stay as we were.

The bulk of the Saracen army had not yet encountered us, a menace marching slowly in our direction. The pagan horsemen regrouped, assembled in a line—a pretty sight, with yellow armor and bright red and blue headcloths, their ranks only slightly reduced. In the near silence we could hear them as they urged their horses forward with gentle kicks, making a clicking sound with their tongues.

This time the Christian archers sent a thick, bright shock of arrows that stunned the attackers, and when they reached us they were already unsteady. I caught a bearded man in the head with twin strokes of my hammer. He went down, hooves gouging his body.

Again, the horsemen fell away.

Our knights called, "Let us at them!" in several languages.

"Wait!" cried King Richard, his fine, black horse snorting, silvery with sweat, his own sword stained with red. "Patience!" he cried, a word nearly the same in Frankish and English.

"Enough patience!" called Sir Nigel.

The enemy riders turned about. They checked their line, smiling, talking to each other. They trotted in our direction.

Nigel gave a laugh of amazement. "Not afraid, are they?"

They began to ride harder, and as they gained momentum Winter Star lifted his head, shivering, laying back his ears.

chapter
THIRTY-NINE

Their warhorses shouldered into us.

Once again Winter Star shuddered, blows striking him as I leaned, working hard with the hammer.

This time when the attack broke off, Rannulf kicked his horse into action, and I followed. It is a squire's duty to keep his knight fit in appearance as well as deed, so I tugged at Rannulf's chain mail where it hitched up behind, and wiped horse foam from his sleeve.

King Richard's horse was nicked in a dozen places, and the king was freckled with blood.

"If we don't take the offensive," said Rannulf, breathing heavily through his helmet slits, "we will have to yield the ground."

"Hold the men back," said Richard, as his personal guard helped lift off his helmet. A dozen hands arranged the bridle, straightened the skirt of blue wool that hung behind the king, wiping a gobbet of pink flesh from his shield. The king's face was aglow. "We are waiting for his reinforcements to get within striking distance."

Rannulf's face was barely visible behind the cross slit of his helmet. The sunlight fell into the dark interior, and a flesh-bright cross illuminated his eyes. "My lord king, it's impossible to keep the men in place."

"They will stay as they are," said King Richard.

It was Sir Nigel who first broke the line.

He was the first to charge after the horsemen, after their next attack, cutting about him with his sword. For an instant his lone figure, with Hubert in pursuit, were the only Christians on the battle-churned field.

At first the pagan horsemen spurred their mounts all the harder, hearing Nigel's battle yell. But it became clear to even the most fight-worn heathen that a sole knight and his squire were all that harried them. The enemy turned, scimitars clashing with Nigel, his sword flashing in the sunlight.

With a roar, up and down the line, our knights broke rank, a lunging wave of horse and man. Bowman were in the way, and what remained of the cheveux-de-frix impeded our attack.

We swept forward, the king riding hard through the turmoil, holding his blade high. Making the best of a bad surprise, he led us in our charge. For a long moment we were a thing of beauty again, the our horses neck and neck, lances at the ready, knights braced for impact.

The Saracen army collapsed. Scarlet-garbed captains called out orders, and noble pagans struck hard at us, secretaries and pages scurrying away from the battle as though that had been the plan all along, a panic so well executed there was little confusion. Even the slain toppled as though by prearrangement, a limb severed, a head lopped, a herd purchased for slaughter.

I buried my hammer in the skull of a horse, and wrenched, unable to free the weapon. With one hand I raised my shield, while my other hand lost its grip, the handle of my weapon slimy with red. I seized a Saracen by the headcloth, and grappled with him, trying to take his sword. The crescent blade arced and wheeled, and Winter Star crumpled under me.

My opponent cut at me, and missed. Pike thrusts from a dozen English soldiers bloodied him, and he dropped.

Winter Star was on his feet again, his entrails dragging.

I pried my hammer from the red mire that covered the ground. I clutched at Winter Star's bridle, and he fell forward, lurching, sprawling heavily to his side.

chapter
FORTY

Some dawns as a boy I would stay snug under a hairy wool blanket while my mother pumped the bellows at the hearth, the room filling with the fragrance of oakwood smoke. I lay quiet those crisp mornings, rain soothing the thatch overhead.

Now I felt suffocated. I could not imagine cold. I could not imagine, except as a faded image, green moss, or long mornings of small rain, the breath of man and beast bright in the winter light. Surely, I thought, I will close my eyes—and Winter Star will be whole again.

But he was no longer trembling, pawing the air with one hoof. He was not breathing.

A rough quiet fell, squires calling the names of their masters, a loud voice in a language I did not recognize demanding attention far at the edge of the field.

I knelt, holding Winter Star's bridle.

Father Joseph once told a miracle story, a wife who was turned into a pillar of salt. It did not sound like such a misfortune to me now. I wished I could turn into a mineral at that moment, some stone that could feel no sorrow.

———

I wept, and then I left Winter Star, flies thick around his wounds.

So many knights and squires were missing it was hard to feel concerned for Hubert and Nigel. In my search of the stunned battlefield I was offered wine from a Turkish goblet, a thing of beauty, sweet to the hand. I was offered captured silk, a bright bolt of orange cloth. One pikeman, his head bound in bloody linen, called me *sire*.

His accent reminded me of home, and he told me he was Osbert, a flock-puller from Copmanthorp. "And as strong a pair of hands you'll never see, my lord. Or as good a wine as this."

The wine was sweet. I paused, took a breath, and drank hard. "Thank you, Osbert," I said. "But I am no lord or knight."

Osbert unwrapped a pigeon's egg, amazingly white and intact in the midst of this carnage, and an emir's finger—he swore that's what it was—both of which I declined with thanks.

I handed him back the sack of wine, and spat a goat hair from my tongue. An English squire put a Saracen headdress over his own cropped scalp, and looked to us to confirm his pride of ownership.

Rannulf was carrying an armload of scimitars, Saracen spurs and bridle bits dangling. His helmet was gone, and when told him I would find it he gasped, "No more need for it today."

"Come with me to find Sir Nigel and Hubert, my lord."

"Nigel?" he asked, as though he could scarcely recall the man. "The man has always wanted this." Rannulf was bleeding from the nose. He sniffed, like someone with a wet cold in the head.

"Surely the two of them can avoid trouble," I said with a confidence I did not quite feel.

"Trouble," said Rannulf, the way a scholar savors an idea. "Avoid it or not, Nigel will be pleased."

"Are you hurt, my lord?"

Rannulf laughed. It was silent lift and fall of his shoulders, and it kept him from doing more than shaking his head.

I felt a tingle of annoyance with Rannulf's exhaustion. I gave a waterboy a carnelian ring I had tugged from a pagan finger, in exchange for sitting with Sir Rannulf and waving flies away from his face with a scarf.

Not all horses had died as peacefully as Winter Star. Some lay with their legs sticking up toward the sky, bellies already swelling in the late-day heat. Others stood shaking, black with blood, half flayed. Many more horses had died than men.

The corpses of the Infidel were strewn, hacked and thick with a breed of fly I had not seen before, an emerald-bright insect in great swarms. Nearly all the dead men were heathen, although word was that a great Frankish knight called James of Avesnes was dead with fifteen Saracens cut to pieces around him.

King Richard had established a column of foot soldiers, and a picket of sharpened staves. The king's voice was clear, ordering the archers and crossbowmen into place.

The Saracen army had withdrawn, a line of men and heaped war-stuff far to the south.

Our own baggage train was scattered. A hooper stood among the remains of a smashed wine barrel. He reminded me of my father, sorting the barrel staves into whole pieces, which could be salvaged, and broken ones, fit for kindling. The sweet decay of red wine filled the air.

Wensten was remarkably unsullied, his tunic pale as a priest's surplice, except for a drying splotch of blood on his chest. He probed the growing pile of battle trophies with a carefree air, a man at a fair with a fat purse.

He wasn't wounded himself, he explained. Turkish raiders attacked the baggage train during the battle, and Wenstan drove off the attackers with his sword.

"No need for concern," Wenstan said, his eyes searching the field. A knight of Sir Nigel's status would be held for ransom, unless he died in the thick of fight. Even a squire would be worth bartering for.

Strong feeling swept me, a feeling for Winter Star too strong to be called simple sorrow, and I took a hard moment to steady myself. The hawk and spit of a carter was loud across the field.

Wenstan loaned me his horse, not a charger, and yet not a mere cob, either, a horse with sensible eyes and a soft mouth. "The Saracen will not respect you if you approach on foot," he said. Wenstan himself straddled a dray horse, a huge, flat-hoofed animal, who clopped along behind me to Wenstan's quiet urging.

We could not find them.

chapter
FORTY-ONE

Fox scat is rich with hair, buck spoor with half-digested leaves—otherwise, it is all the same to me. Even so, I had little trouble following the hoofprints of a dozen horses. Wenstan pointed out the large hoofprints of our English horseshoes, and the smaller prints of the Saracan mounts.

Sunset approached, birds chorusing in the gray-green shrubs that grace the Holy Land. I called out their names, and there was no answer.

Blood told an incomplete tale, a small pond of it, already black and curling at the edges. A spear had broken, the shaft lying on the ground. I slipped from my horse, and hunted through the dry grass.

"You see, there was a fight," said Wenstan. "And the two of them made meat of at least one horseman."

The sound of a carrion bird distracted us, a croak far across the plain.

A pair of wings took to the air.

I could not keep my limbs from trembling, as though all through the battle some power had stored up in me, and now it could escape my body.

We came upon Sir Nigel and Hubert far from the battlefield. Nigel was sitting with his bare arms in his lap, a palsy in his hands, shivering with a sweaty chill.

Hubert leaped to his feet, sword in hand, before he recognized us.

Hubert told the story fast and with spirit, a good chase, a noble fight, mortal wounds for every pagan who wanted one. Sir Nigel had fallen from his horse as the charger stumbled.

Wenstan knelt before his master. As they conferred, head to head, Nigel leaned into his manservant's shoulder with a sigh. "I wanted hostages," Nigel said in a ragged voice. "For silver."

Strong feeling for Sir Nigel made my voice husky. I said, "Hubert, I thought you were food for the birds."

"They tasted us—we needed salt," said my friend.

I doubted that Nigel would survive the journey back to camp.

I led the dray horse, Nigel astride, cradling his shattered arms.

He denied that he was in pain. "I saw a miller once who got caught under the grindstone, arm and thigh," said Nigel. "And he felt no more pain than a wooden angel, until they took to move him."

A brace of Saracen warriors worked the rubble along the battlefield, searching like harvesters for the faces of friends among the slain. At the sight of us, a few of the men took to their mounts, ready to fight or to flee, and I observed this activity with enough concern to make me wish we were somewhere far away. But one of the leaders lifted a hand and spoke to his men, and I recognized the warrior who had watered his horse at the stream—it seemed so long ago.

But the Saracen made no sign of recognition, and I told myself I was mistaken. This was surely some other man—there were so many of the enemy, and I was not able to tell one from another.

chapter
FORTY-TWO

The sea wind was cool.

The beach was crowded, sick and wounded on cots, on crutches, coils of cordage and kegs of pork just arrived, stacked along the sand.

Somewhere down the beach, Wenstan's voice was lifted in song, "Now His body with scourges beat, and His blood so wide out-let." He had begged leave from Sir Nigel to stay in the Holy Land as a servant to Father Urbino, and now I rarely saw the happy manservant, but only heard him, his songs more and more holy, almost always about Jesus' wounds.

A dark Genoese ship lay within bow shot, her keel on the sandy bottom. Sailors called, joking with old friends, and new passengers were floated on board, or helped out to the ship by their companions.

Sir Nigel, his arms in splints, strode into the foam. "Foolish to look so sad, Edmund," he called with a laugh. "You'll be home by winter, or I'm a Mussulman."

He would not let us see the tears in his eyes as he leaned into the easy waves.

"In Heaven's hands," he called.

Only when he was hoisted into the ship by several other men did Sir Nigel turn his face back to us again. He no longer had the fever that had made us despair of him, all those nights. Rannulf had said his bones would heal when he found himself in a place with beef and bread that were not alive with bugs.

It was a bitter surrender for Sir Nigel—he would never see the inside of Jerusalem. And for the rest of the army, who would fight unaccompanied by Sir Nigel, the Holy City seemed much farther away. Hubert's duty was with Nigel, and he had to depart with his lord.

Rannulf leaned on a lance or a staff ever since Arsuf. He said that he could arrange for me to stay here and fight beside some other knight—many had lost squires in the battle. When I asked why he wanted to leave King Richard, Rannulf did not respond at once, and said at last that the king had no great need for fighting men of experience.

Hubert and I had work to do, selling Shadow and much of our fighting gear, although I would keep my hammer. The assault on Jerusalem was still several weeks away, at least. Between our army and the city walls lay Saladin's main force. I had made up my mind to do my duty to my lord, Sir Rannulf, and I carried myself proudly lest anyone believe that our departure had any shame attached to it.

I would see the green hills, and the blond-thatched roofs. I'd smell the chimney smoke on an evening, after a day of long rain. I would see my master's widow, Maud, and I would see Elviva. And test whether a returning Crusader, even one who had not set foot in Jerusalem, might have honor enough to win a father's nod.

Seabirds drifted high above us.

I took Shadow on a last ride into the hills, calculating as I rode how many pennies a strong, gentle horse like this would bring. It was a harsh thought, perhaps, but I wished I could exchange the life of this stalwart, placid—characterless—mount for the return of Winter Star.

I wanted to leave this place. But I also wanted to enter the gates of Jerusalem with King Richard. I had no doubt that after many more weeks and months of fighting, the king would win the Holy City.

I had already seen the city of Our Lord in the distance, but I did not expect it just now.

Or perhaps I had. Perhaps I had taken a path in the direction of God's city, without admitting to myself what I was doing. I crested the hill.

I blinked, and looked away. And then I turned my face toward it again—an unworthy face, with a sinner's eyes.

Walls and keeps of white, domes of gold, and spires that lifted their points toward Heaven. At this distance, it was a map-master's glory. Swallows spun and twisted. Cedars swayed in a wind that caressed the city, but did not touch me.

I turned Shadow back, toward the camp. *Stay,* said the song-bird in the amber brush.

I lifted my hand, and held it just so, blocking the sun. I could not make out Hubert or Rannulf in the crowd of humanity along the shore. Our ship lay closer to the sand now, attended by smaller boats.

Beyond that a Venetian war galley backed oars and slowly turned, guarding the way I would travel home.

About This Book

The essential events of this novel really happened. The siege of Acre and the battle of Arsuf were real, and Richard's slaughter of the prisoners actually took place.

In entering the world of this novel I traveled to the site of Acre, where the rugged and impressive walls are still standing. I visited Crusader tombs in England, where the carved stone effigies of long-fallen knights are the best evidence of what fighting men actually wore. I walked the battlements of the island of Rodos, where one of the finest of Crusader fortresses remains largely intact. I didn't realize at the time that I was researching a book—I wanted to learn about these places, and I was very curious about who had fought in these castles and why.

I spent hours and hours in the British Museum and provincial museums throughout Europe sketching Crusader weapons in my notebook. A key moment in my understanding of the Crusades came when I first laid eyes on a fighting hammer. We usually imagine knights battling with picturesque swords or lances, but many Crusaders went into battle with a weapon like a large croquet mallet, made of iron. When I first saw such a weapon, much of the illusion of the glory and pomp of medieval battle vanished

for me. These men were bludgeoning each other. The weird
slowness and bloody exhaustion of such battle became clear to
me as I studied the actual artifacts of their wars.

And of course I have read with relish on the subject, throughout my life, everything from Scott's *Ivanhoe* to Spenser's *Faerie
Queene,* and I especially valued the works of historians such as
John Keegan and Steven Runciman. A few of the books I read
were astonishingly dull—to discover the silver thread of a medieval prayer I would have to read many pages of academic prose.
But the effort was worth it when I discovered the word or phrase
that awakened me to the events of so long ago.

My own family religious background has been Methodist and
Quaker, and my skepticism regarding war is very deep. And yet I
feel the call that war has on young people, how the need for adventure and personal meaning finds its truest expression, for
some, on the battlefield. This terrible paradox—that caring, re-
sponsible individuals can engage in acts of brutality—both baffles
and fascinates me. I respect the faith of these Crusaders, without
loving anything that they did.

Medieval faith strikes me as strikingly unfamiliar. Few con-
temporary Christians see the hand of the Devil in random household mishaps, and imagine demons behind every shrub. Not to
mention elves, and the so-called *longaevi,* the longlivers, wood
spirits who lived for centuries. These beliefs would have been a
part of everyday faith in the 1190s, not as a teaching of the
Church, but as a part of an ordinary persons' view of nature and
the vast, non-human world.

Ballads and stories were very important to the folk in this
novel's era. They had no books, no TV, but I don't believe they
lived barren lives. Just as jokes and urban legends flavor our work
days, so the ballads would have provided humor and music. Some

of the quoted ballads I have made up, others—particularly the religious ones—are authentic.

This novel takes place in an age before most people developed a respect for critical thinking, and before ordinary people had a tradition of self-questioning. Men and women in King Richard's time did not ask themselves what they really thought about war, or about God. They did not usually question their leaders, or the elements of faith they had been taught, as so many of our contemporaries do. If we suddenly found ourselves in the company of a group of Crusaders, we would find them very unlike the people we have known.

But at the same time I discovered how unlike my own friends the characters of this novel are, I began to see that we have not come so far from those brutal times. War still calls to us, and massacres still take place. We still hunger to reach a sacred city, either an actual, real place, or one inside ourselves.

And the journey is still hard. While Edmund is a character out of my imagination, I think of him as one of the many seekers who have traveled before me.